PRAISE FOR HIGH VOLTAGE

"Another classic from Mr. Gumeny. I'll take this Thor over any of the Marvel Thors any day."

— Stephen Schwegler, author of *Perhaps.* and *Gag*

"Brilliantly funny with at least one laugh out loud on every page."

— Ian McClellan, author of *One Undead Step*

"The third installment of the *Exponential Apocalypse* series continues to deliver. I laughed, cried, threw up, cheered, it's got it all! But really, it's just plain fun!"

— some guy on Amazon

ALSO BY THE AUTHOR

HIGH VOLTAGE

AN EXPONENTIAL APOCALYPSE NOVEL
BY EIRIK GUMENY

Jersey Devil Press
www.jerseydevilpress.com

HIGH VOLTAGE

Jersey Devil Press
Red Bank, NJ

www.jerseydevilpress.com

1st Edition

ISBN 978-0-9859062-2-1

For Monica,
the curse of the Unicorn King be damned

"Aim for their power lines!
They're the devil's veins and electricity is his blood."

– "Obsolutely Fabulous," *Futurama*

HIGH VOLTAGE

PROLOGUE:
FOR THOSE OF YOU JUST JOINING US...

"HELLO, BABY I JUST GAVE BIRTH TO, and welcome to the WGN Chicago six o'clock news. I'm your mother, Alison Glover, coming to you live from the fringes of my own burgeoning insanity.

"Our top story tonight is the neverending blackout that seems to have swallowed our city-state – and presumably the entire planet – whole. Sources are still vague as to what caused the power outage, and witchcraft has not been ruled out. It should, of course, be noted that 'sources' are limited to this reporter and this reporter alone, as she has been hiding in the WGN building for nearly two weeks now, ever since the elevators stopped working and everything outside was transformed into rioting and waywardness.

"This, baby, is why I was recently forced to expel you, a tiny human person, from my vagina – without drugs, assistance, or any idea of how to actually do that. This reporter is talking to you now because professional detachment and a monotonous summarizing of recent events are all she knows and there is a good chance she's only moments away from losing her already tenuous grasp on reality. She hasn't seen another human in days, not since your father went out for milk and was immediately mauled by a roving pack of cannibals. This reporter has since barricaded all the doors and windows and has been living entirely off coffee, powered creamer, and stale Pop-Tarts.

"This reporter would have liked to think that after twenty-six and a half apocalypses society would have been prepared for this kind of calamity, but this reporter was apparently very, very wrong. Despite seemingly perpetual asteroid strikes and unstoppable wildfires and at least one invasion of giant space lizards, we've figured out ways to rebuild from nothing but ashes and bones literally dozens of times. And yet, somehow, we can't figure out how to turn the frigging lights back on.

"I mean, for Hiroshi's ever-loving sake, our scientists have cured cancer, figured out how to run cars off trash, and disproven religion! *Religion!* And then some of those very same fallen gods went ahead and disproved *science*, hiring themselves out to work miracles at hourly rates. We have pills that nullify radiation, we can clone a lost arm or an entire lost *person*, and we regularly get into wars with *robots* over *civil freaking rights!* Ghosts walk the motherflipping earth, along with zombies and werewolves and sentient god damned toasters, so why the *fuck* am I still living in the soul-crushing windowlessness of this godforsaken motherfucking *shithole of a news studio?!*

"Ahem.

"This reporter would like to apologize for that outbreak, baby. She's beginning to forget what actual food and human interaction are, she's diapered you with a dead cameraman's underpants, and she fears she's starting to turn you into an even more messed-up person than this world is already going to make you. With a little luck, though, I'll be dead before you're old enough to understand what I'm saying and blame me for being terrible.

"On the other hand, my ranting appears to have lulled your slimy, adorable countenance to sleep. Maybe you'll be able to handle this world after all, small child that lived inside of me for nine months.

"In any event, this is your mother, Alison Glover, for WGN Chicago, signing off. You nap here while I go and eat the rest of the baking soda I found in the back of the fridge this morning."

CHAPTER ONE:
BENJAMIN "MOTHERFUCKIN'" FRANKLIN

BENJAMIN "MOTHERFUCKIN'" FRANKLIN, a hulking mass of bones, dirt, worms, and faded wool long johns, stood on the far side of the entrance ramp to the Samuel Adams brewery. The walking corpse was hurling fireballs recklessly and roaring toward the heavens.

"Oh, come on," grumbled Thor, the fallen Norse God of Thunder, exiting the brewery and discovering the rampaging, incendiary cadaver. "This wasn't here when we got here!"

"Maybe there's a back door," suggested Boudica IX, clone of the Celtic revolutionary, poking her wild mane of red hair through the doorway.

"Yeah, but it's all the way on the other side of the brewery. And this place is huge."

Benjamin "Motherfuckin'" Franklin bellowed incoherently in reply.

Unlike the other Revolutionary War-era politicians running around, Benjamin "Motherfuckin'" Franklin was not a clone. Shortly after a thermonuclear pissing contest between Canada and Switzerland ended the world for the eleventh time and transformed Philadelphia into a burned-out husk of crime and cheesesteak stands[1], Benjamin Franklin's exhumed corpse was moved to Copp's Hill Burying Ground below the tree-city of Boston[2] where he could, presumably, rest in eternal pieces.

Almost immediately, though, the Charles River running beneath the city overflowed from an excess of feces and Yankees fan corpses during a particularly raucous St. Patrick's Day riot-parade. The green dye and Bostonian excrement seeped into Franklin's grave, waking him from the afterlife and transforming him into a monstrous, super-powered nightmare version of himself.

Benjamin "Motherfuckin'" Franklin had been roaming the forest-metropolis of New England ever since, terrorizing anything and everything that crossed his path, or, really, got anywhere within his peripheral vision.

"I think you're going to have to take him out, honeybutt," said Boudica IX, ducking back into the brewery lobby as a fireball exploded above the doorway. "Or we could go back inside and get drunk and hope he goes away."

"No, the only thing they have ready right now is light beer," replied the former Norse god, "and I will never drink light beer. Stay back."

The sky darkened and thunder rumbled, shaking dust from the brewery facade and sending the empty beer bottles littering the tree-borne walkway into a tiny jig. Benjamin Franklin looked up at the roaring sky just in time to take a bolt of lightning squarely between his rotting, hollowed eye sockets.

The colonial inventor giggled.

"OK," said Thor, raising an eyebrow, "that's not supposed to happen."

"Ben Franklin discovered electricity!" shouted a brewery employee, popping his head through a nearby window. "Lightning won't have any effect on him, he's been struck by it too many times!"

Benjamin Franklin's spine glowed blue and he belched atomic bile at the window, the radioactive fluids eating through the glass and brick and the poor bastard standing behind them.

"Holy shit," said Thor, staring at Benjamin "Motherfuckin'" Franklin, his eyes wide.

"It's Franklin's atomic vomit!" shouted a brewery visitor, crouched behind a nearby railing. "No one knows what it is precisely, or how it happened. When he came back, he just had it!"

"That sounds gross."

"It is! But that doesn't mean it —" The man abruptly stopped speaking and started screaming as he was now on fire. So was the railing. And a pigeon that had chosen a truly terrible moment to alight.

"Damn it," grumbled Thor. Cupping his hands around his mouth, he shouted, "If there are any other people hiding in the immediate vicinity of the brewery and this fire-throwing assclown, you should really run away now."

A half-dozen people scrambled from behind garbage cans and benches and fled past the colonial monster, running down the suspended footbridge and toward the wooden skyline of Boston proper.

Out of frustration, and a lack of variety in his distance attacks, Thor struck Franklin with a tremendous bolt of lightning again, scorching the ground and setting a bench and a few overreaching branches on fire. Benjamin Franklin's knees buckled slightly, but he didn't fall. Instead, he came flying toward Thor, riding the jet of flame erupting from his anus.

"Sugarbuns," said Thor, stepping away from the door and pulling his arm back, "you should probably get back. I think this is going to do some property damage."

Boudica IX backed up from the entranceway and found something solid to crouch behind farther inside the lobby. Peering from the far side of the giant marble statue of a drunken Red Sox fan, she watched through the narrow frame of the door as Benjamin "Motherfuckin'" Franklin roared toward her boyfriend, radioactive bile erupting from his mouth and dissolving Thor's clothes and patches of his skin. The thunder god didn't flinch, bringing his fist forward as Franklin neared. The two collided and Benjamin Franklin's head exploded like a watermelon meeting a sledgehammer. The shockwave shattered every window and splintered every wooden plank in the area, rocking the very tree-foundation of the brewery. Boudica IX, for her part, simply fell onto her butt.

Thor, smoking slightly and more than stark naked, small splashes of muscle fiber visible to the world, looked down and said:

"Damn it. Now I have to buy new pants."

"Not so fast there, snickernoodle," commanded Boudica IX, slinking through the porcupined doorway. "You and I aren't done here yet."

"I'm pretty sure we are," said the thunder god slowly, looking at the headless colonial writer, confusion passing over his face. "And those were the only pants I had, and you and Catrina are always telling me I have to wear them when I go out."

"Catrina's not here."

"Well, yeah, but you are."

"Yes," said Boudica IX, pressing herself against her smoldering boyfriend, a smile on her face. "I am." She pushed Thor to the ground.

After Queen Victoria XXX murdered Boudica IX in a fit of frothing rage, Dr. Lee Arahami, a mad roboticist, brought the cloned Celtic leader back to life using science. However, unlike fellow miracles of cybernetics rendered powerless by the global blackout, Boudica IX was not overly reliant on subcutaneous microelectronics to function. There were, in fact, only a few parts of her affected by the geomagnetic superstorm that turned out all the lights.

Lady parts.

Her bones being titanium, though, and the rest of her mostly meat and human tissue, Thor was unable to strike her with lightning to recharge her genitalia, lest he accidentally fatally electrocute her – even if he did only strike her with a little, tiny lightning bolt, as he often offered. Being in the general vicinity of a much larger sky-clapping electrical discharge, however, turned out to be more than enough to jump start her junk.

"Holy criminy," said Boudica IX breathlessly, rolling off the prostrate thunder god and sitting on the scorched sidewalk, "that was worth the wait."

"I am a fucking god," said Thor, sitting up.

"I know, sweetiepoops," she replied, patting him patronizingly on his shoulder. "You don't need to say it every time."

"Hey, let's go get some pancakes," he said, jumping to his feet, his man bits bouncing in the breeze.

"Sure," agreed the redhead, laying her back on the pavement, her pale chest still heaving. "Just give me a couple minutes to catch my breath."

CHAPTER TWO:
MANUAL LABOR

"HEY, HI. THE LIGHT IN MY ROOM isn't working. Can you fix it?"

"Your light doesn't work because none of the lights work. Anywhere."

"I don't follow."

"There's no electricity in the hotel. There's no electricity anywhere in the state, the continent, or the planet. Your light won't work without electricity."

"But it worked yesterday."

"Yesterday the generators worked. Today they don't."

"That doesn't make sense."

"You don't make sense."

"It's really dark in here."

"Have you tried opening the curtains?"

"I have not."

"You should."

"OK. One sec."

The guest in 212 ducked back into his hotel room. Catrina Dalisay, standing in the hallway with a pile of towels under her arm, closed her eyes and pinched the bridge of her nose with her free hand. It was taking every ounce of her self-control not to run down the gaudy carpet and pummel the guest repeatedly with the first blunt object she could find. Or even just the towels if she had to.

"This is such bullshit," she muttered.

Catrina took a deep breath, her expanding chest barely registering beneath the oversized men's polo she was wearing.

"Hey, that worked!" The guest's head reappeared in the hallway. "It's not dark anymore!"

"That's generally how sunlight works."

"Oh, that's sunlight? That's not going to work at night then, is it?"

"Probably not, no," said the exasperated hotel employee. "But who knows when night's going to fall anyway."

"Well, you should. Shouldn't you?"

"No, why would I –"

"Isn't that part of your job?"

"Knowing in intimate detail the prerogatives of a fickle and broken sky?"

"Yes."

"You are aware that even professional astronomers and astrophysicists are unable to explain why the atmosphere changes colors at random and why the sun can rise and set three times in an hour and why we haven't all just died already, right?"

"Yes."

"But you still think I have the answer to that universal mystery. Because I work for a Holiday Inn."

"Yes."

"You're kind of special, aren't you?"

"That's what my mommy likes to say."

"I'm gonna... go now. I've got... towels." Catrina lifted the linens half-heartedly then abruptly turned from the hotel guest and began walking towards the storage closet at the end of the hall.

There had been twenty-six and a half apocalypses to date. Governments were destabilized so often and so unexpectedly that a person could become mayor by walking into a city and asking politely. The accepted course of action for a global thermonuclear war was to close one's windows and wait a few days until the offending parties tuckered themselves out and took a nap. Big-budget summer blockbusters regularly involved two old folks sitting on their porch, drinking lemonade and talking about their grandkids.

The most recent society-shattering shitshow had been a solar superstorm that wiped out most of the electronics in the world. The sun, after a particularly debaucherous evening, had stumbled across the horizon and flipped a giant, geomagnetic middle finger at the earth, detonating nearly every high-voltage transformer and power line on the planet and crippling the single electrical grid that powered North America.

For good measure, this solar mass ejection also knocked out every satellite orbiting Earth, turning every television, GPS, and communications device into an expensive paperweight. Hundreds of researchers and vaguely suicidal tourists in the southern regions of Siberia, the jungles of Africa, Utah, and other desolate, uninhabitable places found themselves stranded, unable to find their way back to civilization, call for help, or order a pizza. Millions of teenagers, unable to text or leave snarky comments on YouTube, suddenly cried out in terror and were suddenly silenced.

The world was plunged back into the Boring Ages overnight. Although this meant very little to anyone, as no one was able to Google when the Boring Ages were or how society got out of them the first time.

Catrina Dalisay was sitting behind the front counter of the Secaucus Holiday Inn, not doing much of anything. In theory she was manning reception, waiting for the phone to ring or for a reservation to come in over the online booking system, but with the generators still not generating and the internet no longer a thing, neither of those options was looking particularly likely. Instead, the tiny Filipina woman was leaning back in her chair, her feet on the computer keyboard, daydreaming about the many ways she could murder the only guest the hotel had had in six weeks.

Halfway through a blood-soaked fantasy involving an ice cream scoop and a walrus, Catrina heard the stairway door slam open. Sliding her legs off the desk and leaning over the counter, she saw Queen Victoria XXX stepping from the threshold, dragging a bright orange steel hand truck behind her. The beautiful, dark-skinned clone of the long-dead British queen was in khakis cinched with a bungee cord and a baggy green Holiday Inn sweatshirt – her scant wardrobe yet another victim of the hotel's powerless washing machines and a dry cleaner that had fallen into a sinkhole a few weeks earlier.

On the hand truck was Chester A. Arthur XVII, the last surviving copy of the former U.S. president and the re-created queen's boyfriend. Normally a serious, well-dressed man of action – one that wouldn't so much as dream of idly riding a hand truck down four flights of stairs – he was nonetheless duct-taped to the orange steel, tightly, and wearing only unrelentingly snug boxer briefs.

Chester A. Arthur XVII – the majority of his body comprised of electronic components after an unfortunate run-in with an arch-nemesis and a hand grenade – looked more than a little uncomfortable with the current situation, like a man kidnapped by Somali pirates and thrown into the back of a speedboat. The LEDs and access panels lining the president's arms and back were dark, the cannon in his chest was silent, and the few bits of skin he had left around his shoulders and thighs were now red and splotchy from numerous previous tapings.

"I can't help but notice you're getting more and more haphazard about my continued well-being, Vicky, specifically as regards transit without willful and repeated injury," said Chester A. Arthur XVII. The acid sac playing the part of his stomach bubbled loudly. "And, while we're on the subject, I don't think that lo mein you gave me was fit for human consumption."

"It probably wasn't," replied an exasperated Queen Victoria XXX, wheeling her boyfriend halfway across the lobby and parking him with his back to the wall. "I found it under the bed. We're basically out of food until Mark gets back."

"Can we address the willful abuse part of my complaint, then?"

"No. You're lucky I didn't throw you down the elevator shaft."

"You know it's not my fault I'm mostly electrical now."

"And it's not mine either! I shouldn't be punished for it!"

"This happened because I saved your life!"

"And I said thank you six months ago!"

"You think I'm enjoying this?"

"You think *I'm* enjoying this?"

"No, I don't! But that wasn't the question!"

The president and the queen continued on like this for a few minutes before Catrina finally realized what was happening.

"You guys can't have sex if he's powered down, can you?" she theorized.

"No," said Queen Victoria XXX, immediately breaking down, tears welling in her eyes. "His hands don't even work."

"Can't you just, you know, take care of things yourself?"

"You think I haven't?! I've gone through more batteries than the girl's dormitory at a boarding school!"

"Is that why none of the flashlights work? We need working flash-lights, Vicky."

"You going to fuck me?"

"I wasn't planning on it, no," stammered Catrina. "I'm not into the ladies."

"Then shut your useless mouth." The cloned monarch sighed. "I'm sorry. I get angry when I'm horny. And thanks to all these dumb emotions I stopped stifling[3], the stuff that doesn't actively involve boning a person I like and respect doesn't hold me over for very long anymore."

"Are you saying you require honest to goodness emotional intimacy in your sex now?"

"This is exactly why I didn't want to be in a real relationship in the first place," mumbled the queen.

Catrina looked at her with lowered eyes for a moment. Then she said, "Thor's only been gone four days."

"And Charlie's capacitors only keep a charge for a day at a time."

"So... it's been three days since you got any."

"Yes."

"And you're this angry."

"Yes."

"You may have a problem, Vicky."

"It's only a problem when it's not happening," growled Queen Victoria XXX.

"Can one of you scratch my nose?" asked Chester A. Arthur XVII, awkwardly scrunching his face, the one part of himself he still had complete control over.

"Seriously, Charlie?" replied Queen Victoria XXX.

"Please? It's really itchy. I think something bit me."

The reconstructed royal growled. "Do you have to put up with this?" she asked Catrina, waving a hand at the cyborg and walking across the candlelit lobby toward the front desk.

"You mean with Ali?" the girl at the counter clarified. "No, he's doing all right."

"The solar storm didn't affect him?"

"Not really. I mean, his right arm is literally dead weight now, but between the lack of customers and nothing in his store working anyway, it's less of a problem than you'd think."

"I'm not asking about his arm."

"I figured. I'm afraid of what might happen if I start talking about it, though." The hotel clerk blushed. "But, uh, yeah, it works⁴."

"So why isn't he here right now, banging your brains out?"

Catrina stared at her cloned friend, a look of concern on her face.

"OK, all right, I'm sorry," said Queen Victoria XXX. "I'll try to listen to your pointless non-sexy-times story."

Catrina continued to stare.

"No, seriously, I'm fine. Continue."

"Ali's out with Mark and Timmy. Timmy convinced them to turn the grocery run into a peanut butter run."

"That seems destined to end in failure."

"Yeah, well, Timmy was pretty insistent. He said it was 'for his kids.'"

"Yeah, right," the queen scoffed. "All he's been talking about for the last month is peanut butter. I think that squirrel has a problem."

Catrina once more stared at Queen Victoria XXX, a whole new look of concern on her face.

"God damn it, you're right," said the reconstituted monarch. "I should just man up and take care of myself myself. Again." She continued, mumbling, "Then maybe I can look at people without imagining what they look like naked and tied to a bed."

"What?"

"Nothing, nothing," said Queen Victoria XXX. "I'm gonna go upstairs and get my head right."

"I think it's for the best."

"OK."

Queen Victoria XXX continued to stand before the candle-lined front counter, arms crossed and staring vacantly at the ponytailed hotel employee in the oversized shirt.

"Why are you still here?" asked Catrina.

"Oh, am I?" replied the queen.

"It's unnerving when you look at me all empty-eyed like that. You are a very intimidating person, Vicky."

"Right, sorry." Queen Victoria XXX moved her gaze to the floor.

After a moment, Catrina said, "You want me to come with you, don't you?"

"Maybe."

The hotel clerk sighed. "OK, fine. I will hold your hand and tell you you're pretty, but I'm leaving as soon as it gets graphic."

"Thank you."

The two women crossed the lobby for the stairwell, passing the immobile Chester A. Arthur XVII. Queen Victoria XXX repeatedly tried to take Catrina's hand in hers.

"You two are going to return soon, right?" he queried. The stairwell door slammed shut in reply. Chester A. Arthur XVII frowned slightly.

"Now my knee's itchy."

CHAPTER THREE:
SUCK MY BALLS, RACISTS

TIMMY WAS A CHEMICALLY-ENHANCED, telepathic squirrel. As such, he not only enjoyed himself some peanut butter, but he understood that he enjoyed himself some peanut butter and knew how to go about getting more peanut butter so that he could continue to keep enjoying said peanut butter. Lately however, he had been enjoying the nut spread too much. Well, no. Timmy hadn't *enjoyed* it in weeks. He just needed it. On a scary, compulsive level.

To be fair, this unquenchable desire wasn't entirely Timmy's fault. Six months earlier, Nikola Tesla's earthquake machine nearly broke the world in half. While the doomsday device was stopped before it could permanently scar the planet too much, one of the many other consequences of the day was that an offshore peanut butter processing facility got tossed around pretty hard, and the managing company's nicotine and heroin processing operations got mixed up with the peanut butter. Consolidated Phukital, the company in question, did some quick and questionable math, decided the nicotine and heroin levels in the peanut butter weren't high enough to be of concern, and shipped the tainted product off to their customers.

The problem, of course, was that Consolidated Phukital used numbers relating to the tolerance of the average human in their calculations. They did not take into account the effects of heroin- and nicotine-laced peanut butter on a squirrel that stood less than a foot high, even in the gaudiest platform shoes he owned.

Further complicating things, a week after the earthquake the entire world's peanut crop died in an unrelated spontaneous extinction.

The end result was that Timmy the telepathic squirrel was addicted to a product that no longer existed. In no small part because he had eaten a significant percentage of it.

This is how Mark Hughes, Ali Şahin, and Timmy the super-squirrel found themselves in an empty, darkened Piggly Wiggly in the southernest part of what was once Virginia, looking for jars of nut spread.

"Come on, man," thought Timmy, scampering through the surprisingly well-stocked shelves. "Don't hold out on me."

"Timmy, you have to give this up," said Mark, cyborg owner of the Secaucus Holiday Inn and current chauffeur and regretful enabler to a junkie super-squirrel. "This isn't healthy."

"Fuck you!" replied Timmy. "There's got to be some peanut butter here somewhere!" The tiny rodent shoved a half dozen boxes of instant oatmeal to the ground and ran farther down the shelf.

"Timmy! Come on!"

The sounds of a fire door creaking open and slamming shut echoed through the supermarket, a cold breeze carrying the noises down the aisles.

"Can we get out of here?" asked Ali, mechanically-enhanced boyfriend to Catrina Dalisay and owner of the Dunkin Donuts that neighbored Mark's hotel.

"Why, you scared of the dark?" replied Mark. "This blackout must be making things difficult for you."

"It's not the dark." The brown-skinned young man pointed his good hand toward the ceiling, specifically toward the flag of the Confederated Hillpersons of Whitesylvania flapping from the rafters.

"Oh," said the hotel proprietor. "Shit. I didn't think we were that far south."

"Well, we are and I would like to leave."

"I would like to now as well."

"You fellers ain't goin' nowhere," came a voice from behind the men.

"Damn it," said Mark with no small amount of exasperation. He and Ali turned, finding themselves face-to-face with a particularly inbred-looking hillperson, dressed in bleached denim overalls and a poorly-woven straw hat.

"Y'all need to leave," said the hillperson.

"That was what we were planning on doing," said Ali.

"Y'all ain't doing nothin'!"

"Hold on, I'm confused," said Mark. "Do you want us to leave or not? You're contradicting yourself pretty thoroughly."

"Oh, I bet tha's what y'all'd like me t' do."

"Contradict yourself?" said Ali.

"You shut yer filthy mouth, boy."

"We'll be out of here in a second," said Mark, half-assedly waving his hand and turning his back to the hillperson.

"Tha's one second long'r than I'd care t' keep lookin' at you and yer... *friend.*"

Mark rolled his non-mechanical eye and turned back around. "If you're going to say something horrible and racist, just fucking say it. All this dancing around the fact that you're an intrinsically awful person is tiring."

"Oh, well, OK, fine," said the hillperson, somewhat taken aback. He cleared his throat. Then, as menacingly as he could, he said, "We don't wan' none o' yer kind in here."

Mark and Ali stood silently for a second.

"That's it?" inquired the donut shop owner.

"I expected worse," said the hotel owner.

"Oh, I can do worse," said the hillperson, "you godless, sonuvabitch ni—"

The next sound out of the hillperson's throat was a loud, sickening snap. Mark let go of the inbred racist's head and the man's body slumped to the ground.

"Jesus, Mark," said Ali.

"You're not actually upset about that, are you?"

"Not for the reasons you're thinking, no. You know about the Whitesylvanian hive mind, right?"

"The...? Oh shit."

After the world was ended for the sixteenth time, The Ultrapimp was elected President of the United States of America and promptly rounded up all the white supremacists and other assorted bigots and walled them up in the plague colony of Old Maryland. This effectively ended racism forever.

Except, of course, for within Old Maryland.

Between the flesh-eating diseases and the dinosaurs[5], not many of the intolerant assholes survived for long. The few that did, however, eventually figured out a way to escape and made their way back to their ancestral homeland of the South. Thankfully – for everyone else anyway – this was no longer the South they remembered and the racist sacks of shit were chased away from city after city in a flurry of hurled rocks and cannon fire. They eventually settled in a craggy, isolated section of Virginia, where they were free to hate to their hearts' content.

Shortly after incorporating, the settlement of Whitesylvania seceded from the country's government with little to no opposition. The populace knew secession was a terrible idea and that it would leave the racist dickheads vulnerable and desperate, but allowed it all the same, because, as per the official ballot, "Fuck Whitesylvania."

Sadly, though, the colony of prejudiced douchebags thrived – although, in this case, "thrived" meant "thanks to the inbreeding and diseases they still carried from Old Maryland, degenerated into a shambling collective of drooling, subhuman shitheads that literally shared one mind."

An incoherent hollering could be heard outside the Piggly Wiggly, as dozens of shuffling, spitting hillpersons converged on the supermarket, shouting racial epithets and pounding on the windows with their tattered shoes and sharpened pig bones.

"Damn it, Mark, you woke up the racists," said Ali, turning his head quickly. There were halting movements in the shadows.

"All right, let's get Timmy and get out of here," replied Mark.

The two entrepreneurs began slinking through the aisles of the grocery store, hoping to find their furry friend, or at least some cans of soup that weren't minestrone. Eventually they found the squirrel, covered in peanut butter and weeping into an empty plastic jar. Similarly empty jars surrounded the rodent.

"Timmy?"

"These... these were the last jars of peanut butter in the world," thought the super-squirrel. "And I ate them. I ate them all."

"They might not be the last," began Ali. "There might be –" He was interrupted by a sharp elbow to the ribs. "Right, sorry. Ow."

"I didn't even think twice. I just... I just went for it. I tore them open and shoved my entire head in there. I nearly suffocated," said Timmy, looking up and holding out his tiny, peanut butter-covered paws. "But I didn't care.

"I think I might have a problem, guys."

"It's OK, buddy," said Mark, lifting the squirrel gently into the crook of his arm. "We're here for you."

"Speaking of here for us," said Ali, "shouldn't we be fighting off hordes of illiterate, backwoods hatemongers?"

"Yeah, actually," said the hotel owner, scanning the supermarket with his good eye. "We probably should."

Listening carefully, the men realized that the shouting and banging had now turned into screaming and pleading. Before the Whitesylvanians had been able to enter the Piggly Wiggly, they were beset by marauding cannibals. Ali, Mark, and Timmy could see the carnage through the blood-streaked windows.

"Well, that was lucky," said the donut maker.

Luck had very little to do with it. As it turns out, racists taste delicious.

"Can we go home now?" Timmy asked weakly.

"Absolutely, buddy," said Mark, gently stroking the rodent's back.

CHAPTER FOUR:
VERY SENSUAL LEMONADE

IN THE ABSENCE OF ELECTRICITY, the Savoy Bistro, a small French restaurant on the outskirts of the floating city of New New Orleans, had laid out dozens and dozens of candles of various shapes, sizes, and scents. On the tables, on the dividers, on the chandeliers. The cozy, romantic bistro had become even cozier and more romantic than the owners had ever thought possible. They had turned lemons into some very sensual lemonade. Business was booming.

"Was" being the operative word there.

In the middle of the Savoy Bistro were a Siberian tiger and a polar bear, standing on their hind legs and delicately wiping blood from their fur. The animals were surrounded by the restaurant patrons, all of whom were now deceased. Most of them were in very small pieces.

"Oh, that was simply barrels of fun," said the polar bear.

"Quite," replied the Siberian tiger.

The bear and the tiger were also, in point of fact, deceased. So were "Typhoid" Mary Mallon and Lizbeth "Lizzie" Borden, the two elderly ghosts possessing the predators' corpses.

"Fancy some tea?" asked Mary.

"Oh, yes, that sounds lovely," answered Lizbeth.

"Shall I go ahead and put the kettle on here, or did you want to clear out that Starbucks farther down the boulevard, maybe have ourselves a scone?"

"Let us have it here. I rather like the ambience," replied the polar bear, clearing the lower half of a man from a nearby booth. "We can pay our visit to the coffee shop tomorrow morning, during the morning rush."

"I do so love the way you think, Lizzie," cooed the tiger.

CHAPTER FIVE:
CLINICALLY INSANE LIKE A FOX

THERE WAS A HOST OF SAFE, ETHICAL, economically viable alternative energy sources around – wind, solar, nuclear, coked-up hamsters – as well as any number of dangerous, unethical, completely unfeasible ones. The fact nevertheless remained that most North Americans were as lazy and unthinking as a career congressman and chose the power supply of least resistance, attaching their homes and businesses to one of the many high-voltage distribution lines crisscrossing the continent. The electricity was convenient and, without a governing body to regulate the dispersion, it was free[6].

When the North American electrical grid was kneecapped by the geomagnetic solar storm and went offline, however, people slowly realized that their heretofore beloved lack of governmental oversight also meant that no one was coming to fix what was increasingly becoming a catastrophic problem. The credit-based economy was nonexistent[7], hospitals were jamming patients full of morphine and hoping they didn't notice none of their life-support machines were working, and those little coffee makers in hotel rooms didn't do shit anymore.

So, with civilization on the brink of collapse, folks finally decided to get creative.

Sometimes this meant running a refrigerator off an outboard motor. Sometimes this meant flagging down the crazy old neighbor with a shed full of Leyden jars and hoping he didn't ask for anything too creepy or sordid in return. And sometimes this meant laying out some uncharged makeshift batteries, sending a carrier pigeon to the city of Secaucus (in what was formerly New Jersey), and hoping that the fallen deity residing there was able to decipher what "BOSTON NEED LIGHTNING MAN" meant.

Thor Odinson, former Norse God of Thunder, and Boudica IX, the genetically re-created and titanium-reinforced Celtic queen, trudged south along the abandoned interstate. With desolate, brown chaparral flanking both sides of the road, Thor's unkempt beard and hair were easily the most lush growth for miles, save for maybe his girlfriend's wild red mane. The beard, incidentally, was a direct result of his slide back toward true godhood. The more of his former power that Thor reclaimed – which, paradoxically, matched how accustomed he was to humanity – the fuller and more magnificent he and his facial hair got.

Thor adjusted the duffel bag slung across his shoulder, rattling the bottles of beer he had accepted as payment from various Bostonian breweries. His new flannel shirt itched against the patches of raw skin checkered across his hefty body, the cuffs of his cargo pants dragged on the ground, and his sneakers were one size too small to actually be referred to as comfortable. Beside him, the sprite-like Boudica IX fidgeted and danced her way along the highway in Chuck Taylors and a t-shirt held together with safety pins, trying to keep the bare legs beneath her miniskirt from being assaulted by the stray reinforcing bars and vegetation poking through the cracked asphalt.

"Boston and Secaucus seem a lot farther apart than I remember," said Thor. "It didn't take this long going up there, did it?"

"I think we took a different road last time," replied the redhead. "That one had more thorny things and less itchy things."

"Are you sure? Why don't I remember that?"

"Because you didn't fall into the thorny things wearing a skirt."

Thor stared down the never-ending expanse of broken road before him, towards the rapidly setting sun, the reaching brambles and weeds and derelict road signs and disconnected telephone poles all silhouetted against the deepening pink horizon.

"This is bullshit."

"Can't you fly?" asked Boudica IX, yanking her very white leg free of a particularly grabby patch of poison ivy. "Shouldn't that be a thing you can do?"

"No dice, pumpkincans," replied Thor. "Flying is not in my preparatory."

"That doesn't sound right."

"Reparations?"

"No, I meant the flying thing."

"Oh, that. Yeah, no. I can't do that."

"Are you sure?"

"I'm sure. I actually tried it once. I ended up falling four stories, right off the hotel roof and onto some dude's RV. Now I'm not allowed to go back up there."

"I think you might have gotten shafted there."

"I know. The roof's awesome."

"The flying, babycakes."

"Oh, yeah." Thor shrugged. "I don't know, I've never been able to fly. No one in my family could, actually. We did have flying goats, though; Tanny and Tanny Jr."

"Your *goats* could fly but you couldn't? What the heck kind of cut-rate religion were you part of?"

"Loki could turn into birds and bugs and stuff, but he mostly only used it to bother you in the bathhouses."

"That seems like a waste."

"He was kind of an asshole."

"Do you know what happened to him? After you guys fell?"

"I'm not sure," said Thor, walking around a massive hill of massive fire ants. "We didn't exactly get along. Dad said he got a job as a senator, but no one's heard from him since the government was blown up. I'd have to assume he was murdered during the ensuing riots."

"That's kind of a terrible thing to just assume."

"I don't think you understand how much of an asshole he was."

"Hey, you can throw things really far, right?" Boudica IX inquired abruptly.

"Yeah..."

"If you threw something, but held onto it afterwards, do you think you could throw yourself along with it? You know, fake-fly?"

"I don't know, maybe." The thunder god started looking around. "Do you have anything to throw?"

"What about your bag?"

"That's got the beer in it. I don't want to break the beer."

"Then let's drink the beer."

"Yes," said Thor, his eyes wide, "let's do that."

***

Several dozen empty bottles of Ipswich Ale and Wahlberg Bros. IPA littered the ground surrounding Thor and Boudica IX. A few feet in front of them lay the duffel bag, unzipped and sprawled on the asphalt.

"Now it's too light to throw," grumbled the thunder god.

"But did you try *really* throwing it?" the redhead questioned, swaying slightly.

"You are insultingly lightweight for an Irish person."

"I'm not Irish, you horsebutt!"

There was a rustling off to the side of the couple.

"Was that you?" asked the cloned warrior-queen.

"No."

"OK. Hang on a sec." Boudica IX rushed off into the undergrowth bordering the road, returning a moment later with a fox and a pretty wicked rash on her bare calves.

"Here," she said, trying to hold the squirming animal, "you can throw him."

Thor furrowed his brow.

"It's OK, go for it. Animals can't feel pain."

"Timmy's told me otherwise," said Thor.

"Yes, but Timmy also talks with his *brain*. I don't think he counts."

"He's gonna yell at me if he finds out and he can get really mean."

"You're afraid of a squirrel? What're you, a man or a... acorn, I guess."

"Now you're getting mean."

"OK, look." The redhead sighed. "Here's the truth," said Boudica IX, still hugging the wriggling fox, "I am running out of things to talk to you about. All I've got left are a couple really gross stories that even I don't want to know I know. Sacrificing this fox seems worth it to save my dignity."

"Sugarsnatch, I don't think a couple stories —"

"This one time, while I was working with Andy, he walked in on me while I was taking a dump and I ended up letting him —"

Thor grabbed the squirming canine from Boudica IX with his right hand, holding the fox like a football. With his free arm he grabbed Boudica IX around the waist.

"OK, hang on. And please don't ever finish that story."

The thunder god threw the fox mightily, letting go of the animal just long enough to move his grip from its ribcage to its tail. The fox went sailing through the sky, miles down the road, into the hot pink dusk. The tail remained in Thor's hand.

"See, now I feel bad," he said, looking at the furry appendage still in his grip.

"No, it's cool, it wasn't very smart," said Boudica IX. "I saw it eating its own poops. I don't think it was going to last very long on its own. Hey, kind of like Andy."

"Damn it, Bo."

"Well, that's not really fair, Andy didn't eat his *own* poo."

"Please stop talking."

"And it's not like he ate it on purpose, either, it just happened while he was —"

Thor clamped his hands over his ears with tremendous vigor and hastiness, the ensuing percussion inadvertently rupturing his own eardrums. Wincing slightly from the pain, he watched as Boudica IX continued to mime obscenely. Eventually he smiled, realizing that he no longer had any idea what she was saying[8].

***

Mark Hughes and Ali Şahin, meanwhile, were flying back from the Confederated Hillpersons of Whitesylvania on the wings of atomic-powered jetpacks, scavenged groceries in hand and twitching rodent in satchel, making excellent time and each blissfully unaware of what the other was saying.

CHAPTER SIX:
SOMEONE CALL BETTY FORD

MARK ENTERED HIS HOTEL'S LOBBY through the half-boarded front doors, cradling Timmy the detoxing super-squirrel in his arms. Ali was still in the plaza, a few steps behind them, laden with their non-perishable canned good bounty and fighting to disentangle himself from his jetpack, all despite the fact that one of his arms was a cybernetic implant and, due to complications from the geomagnetic superstorm, currently didn't work.

"Timmy!" cried Catrina, rushing across the lobby to her manager's side.

"He's almost through the worst of it," explained Mark.

"What happened?"

"He quit the peanut butter, cold turkey."

"By the scruffy beard of Odin," said Catrina softly.

Mark looked at her with an upturned eyebrow.

"Thor explained to me a while ago that every time I said 'Oh god,' there was no way to prove I wasn't talking about him. So I had to get more specific."

Mark nodded in agreement. "That's actually a good idea."

"Is he going to be OK?" asked Catrina, taking Timmy into her arms.

"Yeah, he'll be fine. At this point he just needs rest."

Timmy scratched violently at his furry arms, twisting and turning in the crook of Catrina's forearm.

"Probably a lot of rest," continued Mark. "Might not hurt to lock his door, too."

Catrina turned and began walking toward the stairwell on the far side of the lobby. Over her shoulder, Mark could see Queen Victoria XXX curled in the fetal position at the feet of Chester A. Arthur XVII, singing weakly to herself. The president, for his part, was staring vacantly across the hotel with glassy eyes.

"What's their problem?" asked Mark.

"They can't have sex," answered Catrina.

"Those poor bastards."

Outside the hotel doors there was a thud and a clatter. A half dozen cans of corn rolled through the doorway.

"Little help, guys?" called Ali.

CHAPTER SEVEN:
UNDERPANTS JUST SLOW HIM DOWN

"OK, I TIED MY BELT TO THIS CINDER BLOCK," said Thor, his hearing mostly restored. He and Boudica IX, once again completely sober, were still lost somewhere in the scrub-strewn wasteland between Boston and Secaucus. "Let's see if this works."

Boudica IX was wrapped around the thunder god – her legs around his waist, her arms around his neck, her nose in his ear.

"OK, I'm ready," she said.

Thor wrapped one end of the belt tightly around his knuckles, the steel-reinforced pleather going taut between his hand and the concrete on the ground just behind his feet.

"I hope my pants stay up," he said.

"Maybe next time you should buy the ones that I pick out for you," replied Thor's girlfriend. "You know, the ones that fit."

"Never."

Swinging his arm forward, the fallen thunder god hurled the cinder block into the light brown sky, the belt straightening and stretching, digging into his palm, and then yanking Thor from the ground. He and Boudica IX followed the arc of the concrete, effectively flying over the nature-ravaged highway.

"Holy shit," cried Thor, wind whipping past his face, "it's working."

"Woo!" cried Boudica IX, leaning her head backward into the rushing air.

The duo sailed over the old interstate for a few more minutes, marveling at the scenery and only occasionally screaming that plausible physics could suck it. The cinder block reached the apex of its parabolic flight and began its return trip to the earth. This was not something the god nor the Celtic queen was prepared for.

"So, uh, we're just falling now, aren't we?" asked Boudica IX.

"Yeah, I don't really know how to land this thing," replied Thor.

"At least it's open space, right? It's not like there's a –"

"Bridge!"

Thor let go of his belt and wrapped his arms around Boudica IX, twisting in midair and turning his back toward the approaching overpass. The cinder block shattered against the abandoned bridge, while Thor tumbled through the overpass like a brick through a sheet cake.

After a few moments of uncontrollable rolling, the thunder god and the clone came to a stop and lay on their backs in the rubble, staring into the darkening chocolate sky. They sat up as one, shaking their heads and brushing dirt and debris from their persons. It was then that they realized Thor's cargo pants did not make the trip with them.

"Don't say anything," grumbled the thunder god.

"I won't," said Boudica IX, unweaving a tiny chunk of asphalt from deep within the depths of her red hair. "But why didn't you buy underpants?"

CHAPTER EIGHT:
RIB TICKLIN'

THE SECURITY OFFICER THUDDED AGAINST the sidewalk in a rain of broken glass. His intestines followed soon after.

"Typhoid" Mary Mallon, now possessing the remarkably well-preserved body of professional wrestler James "The Ultimate Warrior" Hellwig, stood inside the disheveled Dickey's Barbeque Pit, glowering through the shattered window at the man who had been foolish enough to try to get between her and her unceasing thirst for bloodshed.

Mary paused to think about that for a moment. While it was certainly true that the security officer was trying to stop her, he ultimately ended up very dead and had little to no impact on her marauding. If anything, she realized, the man had, in point of fact, *helped*, adding yet another bloody statistic to her already impressive body count.

Mary stopped glowering and instead curtsied to the man, the body of The Ultimate Warrior daintily bobbing, his massive wrists lightly upturned.

"Thank you, sir," she said to the corpse. "I do appreciate your support."

Mary then turned around and snapped the neck of another security officer who had been frantically hitting her with a nightstick for the last few minutes.

Looking up from the twitching cadaver at her feet, Mary saw Lizbeth "Lizzie" Borden, now possessing a blood-soaked wendigo[9], slump down at one of the picnic tables lined across the barbecue restaurant and slide a large plate of ribs before herself. Whether the ribs were animal or human was unclear.

"My goodness, I am famished," said Lizbeth in a guttural growl, before immediately biting into a rack of barbecued meat, bone and all.

Mary delicately sat down opposite her. She flicked some viscera from her bulging bicep.

"This did seem a particularly grueling endeavor, did it not?"

"Perhaps for you," explained Lizbeth before patting her furry chest. "This beast certainly made short work of all challenges."

Mary looked down at her oily pecs and tree trunk legs. She could see very little else. She couldn't help but feel as though she was suffocating within her own muscles.

"You may be right," said Mary eventually. "The aesthetics of this body may be more impressive than their actual capacity for savagery. The arm of that one woman barely came off at all."

"One cannot beat Mother Nature for cruelty."

Mary laughed lightly. "I am not sure a *wendigo* constitutes natural, dear Lizzie."

Lizbeth chortled through a mouthful of ribs.

"Oh, dear me," she said, quickly raising a terrifying clawed hand to her mouth. "Please pardon my manners."

***

A throat was cleared gruffly and deliberately. Lizbeth and Mary, faces covered in barbecue sauce, turned to find a man standing at the end of their table, less than three feet from their elbows. He looked to be about sixty years of age, with shaggy salt-and-pepper hair and dark, sunken eyes, dressed in the most expensive-looking cheap suit either of them had seen in the twenty apocalypses since ghosts had begun walking the earth.

"Ladies," said the grizzled man, bowing slightly, his face as creased as a rotting pumpkin. "I do hope you'll pardon the interruption, but I have a favor to ask of you."

CHAPTER NINE:
THE BEST LAID PLANS OF MICE AND CYBERNETIC HOTEL OWNERS...

A FEW DAYS AND SEVERAL FAR-FLUNG SACKS of highway debris later, Thor and Boudica IX finally returned to the Secaucus Holiday Inn, bedraggled, bruised, and bleeding slightly from various outlying areas.

They never did figure out how to land.

The nights likewise proved to be more difficult, and much colder, than the couple had anticipated. After his attempt at a campfire accidentally burned down several acres of dried-out scrubland, Thor was instead forced to belt a length of moss across his waist to protect his boys from the near-freezing temperatures. Boudica IX, for her part, had created a terrifying, yet incredibly comfy, overcoat, sewn together with twigs and hair and made from the skins of animals too stupid to escape the raging wildfire.

On the plus side, the god and the queen ate extremely well.

Limping through the boarded-up front doors and into the dim, candlelit lobby, Thor was immediately accosted by a sunken-eyed Queen Victoria XXX.

"Hey, Vicky," he said, "how's –"

"No talking," rasped Queen Victoria XXX, shoving Thor back outside with one hand and wheeling a comatose Chester A. Arthur XVII behind her with the other. "You hit this asshole with lightning. Right the fuck now."

"I really have to pee."

The re-created English royal grabbed the thunder god by his filthy beard and pulled his face directly opposite hers. She said nothing.

She only stared.

Thor had not known real fear in his life until that moment, looking into the icy black void of Vicky's soul. His spirit shrank, retreated to his bowels, and stayed there for several days.

"OK," he whimpered, and shuffled to a clear area of the plaza.

"I'm coming too!" shouted the be-animaled Boudica IX, skipping after them.

***

The next afternoon, the entire Holiday Inn gang – Thor Odinson, Boudica IX, Catrina Dalisay, Ali Şahin, Mark Hughes, Timmy the detoxed super-squirrel, Chester A. Arthur XVII, and Queen Victoria XXX – convened in the lobby of the hotel, situating themselves in armchairs and sofas around a single, smallish coffee table in the middle of the room. Thor had recharged the generators and everyone was freshly showered, wearing clean clothes, and sane. The exception to the last two, of course, being Boudica IX, who was still wearing a hollowed-out wolf for a hat.

Charlie and Vicky had appeared last to the gathering – exhausted, glowing, and wearing rumpled gym clothes, despite the washers, dryers, and irons all working again. The cloned president was limping slightly, as parts of him were already starting to shut down.

"Were you guys boning this entire time?" asked Thor.

"Yes," Catrina answered sternly. "They're very loud."

"Did you guys break a lamp or something this morning?" asked Ali.

"It was the television," replied Queen Victoria XXX.

"You guys know those things cost money, right?" Mark inquired. "It's not like they work."

"That's the worst part of this stupid blackout," grumbled the fallen god.

"Really, Thor? No TV's the worst part of this?" said Catrina.

"I guess the lack of cars thing is pretty bad too."

"What lack of cars thing?" Chester A. Arthur XVII raised an eyebrow.

"You know, how they don't work. And we have to walk everywhere."

"Is that why you guys took so long?" asked Queen Victoria XXX.

"We also got lost," added Boudica IX.

Chester A. Arthur XVII sighed. "Any kind of electromagnetic interference, like an EMP or the solar mass ejection that caused this current planetwide clusterfuck, only affects genuine, contained electrical systems. Like the continental grid, or me and my self-inducting closed circuit transformers, since Lee ironically enough didn't want me to have to worry about charging. Automobiles, on the other hand, run on galvanic cell batteries and internal combustion engines. Electromagnetics have zero effect on either of those systems."

"But..." began Thor, "but the TV said cars don't work in a blackout. Everyone's always walking. And stabbing people for magical amulets and gasoline."

"We've been off gasoline for years," said Ali.

"What's gasoline?" asked Catrina.

"Even if we did still have cars that ran on petroleum derivations, it's completely possible to retrieve gasoline from your standard roadside service station with no electricity. Difficult, yes, but not impossible," continued Chester A. Arthur XVII. "And, more importantly, none of that is in any way the car's fault. Any person or television program that tells you otherwise is a terrible, filthy, ignorant, horrible, stupid liar."

"Unless someone's car is one hundred percent electric," said Ali.

"Well, yeah, unless that," said Chester A. Arthur XVII.

"So... TV lied?!" said Thor, alarmed.

"I'm afraid so, buddy," said Mark.

"Besides, you could've just used the nuclear-powered jetpacks," added Queen Victoria XXX.

"We still have those?" asked Thor.

"We have four," Ali answered.

"Wait, hang on..." Thor furrowed his brow and bit his lip. He began staring absently at the arm of the sofa he was sitting on.

The thunder god stared for a while, broken only by bouts of acute blinking. Chester A. Arthur XVII scratched his shoulder. Catrina scratched the back of her neck.

"Is he OK?" Timmy wondered.

"He's just thinking," explained Catrina.

"Oh god," said Queen Victoria XXX. "Should we help him?"

"Give him a second. I think he can do it."

Boudica IX began furiously scratching her chest.

"Something's really itching me," she said.

"That wolf probably had fleas," added Queen Victoria XXX, suppressing the urge to scratch her own chest.

"Animals can't get fleas in the wild," said Timmy.

"Seriously?"

"Yeah," replied the squirrel. "Although there are a hundred other things wrong with wearing the carcass of another animal for fun."

"I really like the way it looks," said Boudica IX softly.

Thor began moving his head slightly and haphazardly, like a slowed-down tic.

"That's probably not good," offered Ali.

"Honeyballs? Are you OK?" inquired Boudica IX, leaning over and putting her arm around the thunder god. "We all know the answer already. We can help you."

A moment passed. Then Thor blurted out, "You mean we didn't have to walk all the way to Boston?!"

Everyone in the room applauded.

"Son of a bitch," continued the former Norse god. "I don't think I've ever been so annoyed. I mean, that trip was so *boring*."

"Dude, your girlfriend is *right there*," said Catrina, pointing toward Boudica IX.

"No, he's right, it devolved pretty quickly," corrected the Celtic queen. "I don't have a lot to talk about and all his Asgard stuff is tedious and confusing."

"Plus her vagina was locked up for most of it so we couldn't even fuck," added Thor.

Boudica IX nodded in agreement, the wolf head bobbling atop her own.

"Why..." began Catrina, only to stop herself. If two people were too dumb to realize they shouldn't be together, should they be told? Or was their ignorance compatibility enough? The questions hung in the air like smoke from a broken toaster oven. The clones, cyborgs, and squirrel all looked at one another and the lobby descended into the most awkward awkward silence in the history of societal discomfort.

Thankfully for everyone, the generators chose that moment to crap out again, throwing a blanket of near total darkness over the group. Faint wisps of orange sunlight snuck through the partially boarded-up front doors.

"Why did you get electricity-powered electrical generators again?" asked Thor.

"They were on sale and I wasn't thinking," Mark explained.

"I'll get the matches," said Catrina, walking behind the front desk.

"I got it," said Chester A. Arthur XVII, utilizing the flamethrower built into his arm and lighting all the nearby candles, as well as scorching most of the wall and causing everyone else in the room to duck. The clone's arm immediately shut down and fell to his side.

"Damn it."

"Why would you even do that?" scolded Queen Victoria XXX. "You knew that would happen."

"It seemed like a good idea at the time."

"Hey, speaking of good ideas," said Mark, "why haven't you guys just fixed the blackout and turned the lights back on for good?"

Everyone's eyes went wide as one.

"Son of a bitch," said Chester A. Arthur XVII.

"How did you not think of that?" asked Queen Victoria XXX, turning toward her partner. She shoved his chest with both hands and he promptly fell off the chair arm on which he was perched.

"Why didn't *you* think of it?" countered the president, pulling himself back up slowly with his one functioning arm. "Or Catrina?"

"Because that's not my job!" shouted Catrina. She tossed a stapler at Chester A. Arthur XVII. It skittered across the carpet, missing entirely.

"We figured that if you didn't suggest it, it must not have been something that we could do," clarified Ali.

"For the better part of the last month, Thor has regularly been striking me with lightning to get my once-deceased body functional for a day or two at a time," explained Chester A. Arthur XVII. "There is no way my brain is performing at the level at which we've all become accustomed. I am blameless in this."

"You're the leader!" shouted Catrina.

"Vicky and Bo are leaders too!"

"You know what I mean!" The clerk hurled a handful of paperclips toward the president. They scattered harmlessly to the floor a few feet from the desk.

"That just seems wasteful," said Mark. "You know we can't vacuum."

"I don't know what I thought would happen there."

CHAPTER TEN:
THE SCOURGE OF ALL MANKIND

"JUST TO CLARIFY, YOUR CAR WORKS?" asked Thor, scratching behind his ear.

"Yes, Thor," replied an exasperated and only barely functional Chester A. Arthur XVII. "The engine and all systems run entirely on methane. I should have enough compressed tanks to get us to Las Máquinas. On the off chance I don't, though..." He turned toward the tiny Filipina hotel employee. "Catrina, you made us some chicken afritada, right? And all the brown rice you could find?"

"Yes, they're in the mini-fridge in the trunk," said Catrina. "I still don't like the sound of this."

"And Ali, you rustled up a dozen or so mason jars? And whatever other vacuum-sealed containers you had in the back of the Dunkin Donuts?" continued the cloned president.

"This is going to get disgusting, isn't it?" replied Ali.

"Almost certainly."

Ali, Catrina, Thor, Queen Victoria XXX, and Boudica IX were standing in the Holiday Inn lobby, near the front doors. Chester A. Arthur XVII was slumped in a corner, as everyone was tired of holding him up. He was at least fifty percent metal and not exactly lightweight. Nearby were several duffel bags of clothes and weapons, and one smaller canvas bag full of nothing but deodorant and air fresheners.

"Right, so you want me to load the rest of this up into the fart car?" asked the thunder god.

"I really hoped we'd be able to get through this without someone actually saying 'fart car,'" said Queen Victoria XXX.

"Wait," began Catrina, turning to Thor. "How'd you know that flatulence was mainly methane? You think burritos are unripe tacos."

"Where do you think all the compressed methane came from?"

Everything within earshot, including a pair of blue jays outside the doorway, groaned in disgust.

"And yet somehow you still didn't know cars worked during a blackout," said Queen Victoria XXX.

"I didn't know what they were *for*. Someone says fart and I say how much."

Everything groaned in disgust again.

In the six years since Chester A. Arthur XVII and his fellow political knockoffs were released from the German sausage company that had created them, the cloned president had developed something of a love/hate relationship with automobiles. Specifically, he loved cars like a developmentally-disabled man-child loved rabbits – working on them, reading about them, talking about them, staring at them longingly – but he hated the way they kept getting taken from him and wrecked. The president's four previous vehicles had been, in chronological order, "borrowed" by his former roommate William H. Taft XLII and driven into a sinkhole, stolen by a suicidal ostrich and driven into a tar pit, stolen by a ghost-possessed zombie cowboy and driven into a tree, and stolen by a two-hundred-year-old Nikola Tesla and driven into a hotel.

Chester A. Arthur XVII decided he would take no chances with this newest car and started from scratch, fabricating the entire vehicle himself from the steel-reinforced tires up and including every safety feature and anti-theft device known to mankind, as well as a few new ones he invented or stole from robots. The frame was made from tungsten carbide, the body from titanium, and the bulletproof windows were fortified with diamond filament. The exterior was painted a scratch-resistant matte black, while the red leather seats were absolutely saturated in a highly toxic stain- and water-repellent of his own design. There were four large caliber cannons worked into the body, and possibly up to six more that Chester A. Arthur XVII refused to acknowledge, most likely for legal reasons. The trunk could fit two large motorcycles and the interior could comfortably seat eight. In truth, the vehicle was more of a luxury tank than a car.

A large part of the design, though Charlie would never admit it, came from Thor's constant assertions to "make a god damned Batmobile."

Queen Victoria XXX maneuvered the custom-built vehicle out of the hotel parking lot and onto the main road around the plaza. Chester A. Arthur XVII was duct-taped to the passenger seat beside her. Catrina and Ali sat in the row behind them, while Thor and Boudica IX occupied the backseat. All of them had cup holders, heated seats, and exceptional legroom.

"So who's paying us again?" asked Thor.

"No one," said Chester A. Arthur XVII.

"Then why are we doing this? Are we being autistic?"

"Altruistic."

"Sure, whatever."

"No," said Queen Victoria XXX. "It's for selfish reasons."

"Oh, OK," said Thor. "That's fine."

"What's the plan, by the way?" inquired Catrina.

"We're going to go talk to Dr. Arahami," explained Chester A. Arthur XVII.

"And then...?"

"Do whatever he says, I guess. Repairing the continental electrical grid is a little out of my wheelhouse."

"That's our entire plan? Trust the mad scientist?" asked Ali.

"How many of your brain cells has Thor electrocuted?" Queen Victoria XXX seconded.

"Lee brought a solid one-third of us back from the dead," said Chester A. Arthur XVII, intending to look at Boudica IX but unable to move his head or neck. "I think we can trust him. Besides, who else is going to know how to repair the North American electrical grid?"

"An electrician?" replied Ali.

"Does anyone know an electrician?"

Everyone looked around, avoiding the gaze Chester A. Arthur XVII was unable to fix them with[10].

"Right. And does anyone have any better ideas?"

"I could strike the entire world with lightning," said the former Norse god, raising his hand. "Like, a lot of lightning."

"I said 'better,' Thor."

"Oh, I didn't hear that."

Ali wriggled in his seat and scratched the underside of his thigh vigorously.

"Easy there, killer," said Catrina with a small laugh. "Did Boudica give you her fleas or something?"

"Hey, that's not fair," a very sad and very offended Boudica IX pouted. "Timmy made me get rid of my wolf cloak." She quietly added, "I really liked my wolf cloak."

"Guys?" asked Queen Victoria XXX, catching a glimpse of a smoking inferno in the rearview mirror. "Do you think Mark knows the hotel is on fire?"

All eyes capable of doing so turned to Thor.

"What? I didn't do that," he said.

"Are you sure?" Catrina narrowed her eyes.

"Did you charge the generators before we left?" asked Chester A. Arthur XVII.

"Yeah, Mark asked me to."

"How many volts did you charge the generators with, Thor?"

"I don't know, a lot. I didn't know how long we'd be gone."

"Their top capacity is only about ten thousand watts. If you went too far in excess of that you would have overloaded them and risked the possibility of starting a fire."

"Oh," said Thor. "Then, yeah, I probably did that."

"Should we go back?" Boudica IX suggested, turning around and staring through the rear window. "Help Mark put it out?"

Thor likewise turned around to look at the growing conflagration. He shrugged.

"He'll figure it out eventually."

"That's our home, guys," said Ali.

"Yeah, but all our *stuff's* in this car," said Thor.

"Not all of it," said Queen Victoria XXX. She unconsciously began to slow the car. "I left my iPod on the nightstand."

"He didn't have to put us up there, you know," said Catrina. "The only thing he's asked from us is that Thor and I keep working there, and, quite frankly, we're terrible employees."

"We are the worst," said Thor.

"We do kind of owe him," said Queen Victoria XXX, scratching absentmindedly at her armpit.

"Are you itchy too?" asked Chester A. Arthur XVII, straining his peripheral vision.

"I used an old razor this morning, I don't think it agreed with me."

"I've been itchy for days," said Catrina.

"The underside of my testicles has been irritated for the last two hours," added Chester A. Arthur XVII.

"Mine too," said Thor, scratching with great abandon. Everyone in the vehicle began to do likewise.

"God damn it," said Catrina. "Did we get fleas?"

"It's not fleas," said Boudica IX sternly.

"Then what the fuck is it?"

"Are rashes contagious?" Ali inquired. "Who got a rash and didn't tell anyone?"

"I always tell you when I get a rash," said Thor.

Boudica IX, in a fit of impassioned scratching, removed her t-shirt, revealing dozens of small red welts across her very white stomach and chest, lined up in groups of three. Thor did the same, revealing the same.

"What the hell?"

"I think the hotel has bedbugs," answered Boudica IX.

Queen Victoria XXX threw the gearshift into park and popped the trunk.

"Everyone out," she ordered. "We're burning our clothes. And towels. And anything and everything else that could possibly harbor those little blood-sucking motherfuckers."

"Is the car going to be OK?" asked Thor. "We're not going to have to walk again, are we?"

"The car's fine," said Chester A. Arthur XVII. "Bedbugs can't survive in leather, and the interior's been treated with weapons-grade chemicals anyway."

"Is that why I'm dizzy?" Ali mumbled.

"What about the hotel?" asked Catrina, her door open and her jeans off.

"Fuck the hotel," replied the queen, unclasping her bra. "We would've had to set it on fire anyway."

CHAPTER ELEVEN:
THE CHEETOS! WON'T SOMEBODY PLEASE THINK ABOUT THE CHEETOS?!

TIMMY THE SUPER-SQUIRREL AND HIS WIFE and kids huddled beneath a chair outside the shuttered Dunkin Donuts, watching Mark Hughes, owner of the Secaucus Holiday Inn, stare distraughtly at his burning hotel. Ash fell like filthy snow across the plaza.

"Well, this is unfortunate," the hotelier muttered.

The other residents of the plaza – two Armenian jewelers and one tenacious Greek restaurateur, who had rebuilt her eatery no fewer than three times – gathered behind Mark, staring up at the conflagration and secretly hoping it would consume the whole plaza. Business had not been great lately. The green lights of the Holiday Inn sign sputtered and died, the H, O, and L cannonballing from the building's facade.

A man appeared in a second floor window, banging on the glass and fumbling with the latches, trying to get it open.

"Oh shit," thought Timmy. "212." The squirrel scampered across the brick of the plaza and up Mark's khakis and polo shirt, onto his shoulder.

"We have to get him out," he said to Mark with his mind.

The hotel guest figured out the latches and slid the window open.

"Hey!" he shouted. "It's really hot in here!"

"The building's on fire!" shouted Mark, his hands cupped around his mouth. "Get out of there!"

"The air conditioning doesn't seem to be working!"

"THE HOTEL IS ON FIRE!"

"Does that mean you'll knock today off my bill?"

"We should still probably at least *try* to get him, right?" said Timmy.

"GET OUT OF THERE! THERE'S A LADDER UNDER THE BED!" bellowed Mark.

"All of my ice is melting!" shouted the man.

The hotel manager shrugged. "I feel good about our efforts."

"We did what we could," said Timmy with a tiny sigh.

"Oh fuck," barked Mark suddenly, "Sheila!" He began to run toward the flaming deathtrap that was the hotel.

"Mark, no!" shouted Timmy, digging his claws into the hotel manager's shoulder and throwing all his inconsequential weight backwards. "It's too late! She's gone!"

"No!" Mark swatted Timmy from his shoulder and charged into the cloud of smoke billowing from the front entrance. The squirrel hit the ground hard and rolled, end over end. Timmy's tiny wife turned away, covering the eyes of their even tinier children.

Recovering, Timmy ran halfway toward the hotel, thinking as loudly as he could, "She's not worth it, Mark! Let her go!"

***

Nearly ten minutes passed before Mark reemerged in the collapsed entranceway, coughing and covered in soot and dragging a deformed, melting vending machine behind him.

"I feel like I might be missing something," said Alexa Kostopoulos, owner of the Olympia IV grill and bar, brow furrowed in confusion. "Is Sheila trapped inside the vending machine? Is she a little person or something?"

"Sheila *is* the vending machine," explained Timmy.

"Mark was dating a vending machine."

"Yes."

"He... talked to me about their bedroom problems once."

"Yeah."

"So they..."

"Yep."

"Oh my."

"That's about right."

"I guess that explains why he never brought her over for dinner."

The Greek woman and the squirrel watched as Mark knelt over the warped appliance, weeping and banging his fists and shouting to the heavens while ash continued to rain down around them. A panel on the side of the vending machine buckled and broke loose, spilling a dozen bags of jalapeño potato chips onto the brick plaza. Sobbing, Mark grabbed them and pulled them tightly to his chest.

"That... that's not right," said Alexa.

"That hasn't been right for a while," replied the psychic squirrel.

CHAPTER TWELVE:
THE OMEGA WOMAN

THE ROCKAWAY TOWNSQUARE MALL had seen better days. This wasn't surprising, as the world itself had seen better days and the Rockaway mall was part of the world. Still, even for a large shopping center in a desolate post-post-post-post-post-post-post-post-post-post-post-post-post-post-post-post-post-post-post-post-post-post-post-post-post-apocalyptic wilderness, Rockaway Townsquare was hurting. Of its two hundred stores, only one hundred and twelve were still extant, and, of those, only one was still staffed. The ten-foot-tall lights spelling out "ROCKAWAY" above the mall's main entrance had collapsed in such a way, through sheer chance and the fault of no one in particular, that it now spelled "GO AWAY." And then, of course, there was the fact that the nearby interstate was no longer functional, the surrounding municipalities and parks had been on fire for the better part of two years and were now fields of still-glowing embers threatening to reignite or burn down the mall itself should the winds shift, the parking lot was a literal death trap built to ward off the zombies and homicidal turkeys after the sixth and fifteenth ends of the world respectively, and the mall had officially closed after the twenty-first end of the world – the third apocalypse in a one year span. None of these made for a particularly pleasant or sane shopping experience.

In fact, if it wasn't for the free food, free clothing, free shelter, the seemingly never-ending ICEE machine in the food court, the lack of public transportation, and the inability to locate her family or friends, Ellie Belle would have quit her job at Eddie Bauer and moved away in a heartbeat.

As it was, she hadn't seen another person, much less a customer, in the nearly four years since the mall closed. She had become quite friendly with the pigeons, the smarter rats, and some of the more risqué items for sale in the secret back room of the lingerie store, however, plus she regularly forgot that the people on the televisions in the "Best"

Buy weren't real, so it wasn't all bad. If anything, hers was a life of quiet satisfaction and stability, and she actually kind of enjoyed it.

Which is precisely why – after a booming crack of thunder and the miraculous return of the lights – when six naked, bug-bitten people walked into her outerwear store, Ellie was not ready. She had, in fact, given up on ever being ready and was wearing an empty Popeyes' three-piece takeout box on her head and stained thermal underwear on the rest of her. She was also knuckle-deep in her own nose.

"Hi," said the tallest, blondest, and presumably coldest naked person. "We need clothes."

Ellie, lounging atop the checkout counter, her back against the register, turned slightly, looked them up and down, swung her legs over the edge of the counter and, after clearing her throat for the better part of five minutes and remembering how to talk, said, "OK, sure, go nuts."

She did not remove her finger from her nose.

The sextet of nude folks dispersed throughout the store, rummaging through racks and shelves and piled tables of cargo pants and heavy canvas frocks and leather jackets and thermal-lined flannel shirts and tactical vests and ripstop khakis and wool panties and radiation-resistant boxer-briefs and boots and hiking shoes.

"So," asked Ellie, "is it still just a panorama of desolate, flattened hellscapes everywhere out there?"

"Pretty much," replied the ivory-white red-haired woman, slipping into a heavily-pocketed leather and canvas skirt.

"Are the flying monkeys still a problem?"

The tiny ponytailed woman by a rack of camp shirts raised an eyebrow. "No?"

"Oh," said Ellie, disappointed. "I guess that's good. Hey, does anyone want coffee?"

"I could actually go for one," said the dark-skinned man with the limp metal hand, wriggling his head through the neck of a hooded fleece sweatshirt.

"Cool. It's down the way," explained the salesgirl, pointing to her left. "You can crawl through the hole in the security gate. The Sumatran roast is pretty good."

"Oh, uh, all right," he replied slowly. "Did you want anything?"

"No," said Ellie, admiring the bevy of private parts still on display, "I'm good."

"Don't you have anything less... mountain man?" inquired the dark-skinned woman, holding up a heavily-pocketed vest and grimacing slightly. "Something more form-fitting and bulletproof? Or underwear that doesn't make me look like I've given up on life?"

"That's why I gave up on underwear," said the redhead, her voice muffled by the bulky cable-knit sweater she was swimming through.

"You could try Ashley J. Williams' Fancypants Emporium, or Cobblepot Couture," replied Ellie. "I think they're still standing. There might be wolves, though."

"I'm coming with you," said the handsome mostly-metal white guy, tossing a nylon field jacket back onto the display table.

"What's the matter?" asked the shirtless, broad-shouldered blonde man, a handful of abdominal muscles etched across his belly. "You guys too good for this stuff?"

"Yes."

"We like fancy things, Thor," the raven-haired woman stated. "For whatever reason, our progenitors' fashion sense stuck with us, even if things like ethnicity and their crazy-ass morals didn't."

"That's dumb," said the blonde man.

"You're dumb."

"Really? Then why did I pick these flannel-lined jeans? I've farted twice during this conversation and you didn't hear anything!"

The metal man and the naked woman shook their heads in disgust and walked out of the Eddie Bauer.

"I don't know, I thought it was pretty smart," said Ellie.

CHAPTER THIRTEEN:
IS HEAVEN MISSING AN ANGEL? CAUSE YOU VE GOT NICE CANS

MARK HUGHES SLUMPED IN THE VINYL booth, dejected and filthy and mechanically shoveling fork after fork of cheesecake into his mouth. Lime green sunlight poured through the windows into the powerless diner.

"Come on, Mark," thought Timmy the super-squirrel, sitting on the table before his friend, but off to the side enough that he wouldn't accidentally get stabbed with the fork, "you can't keep doing this. This is your third cheesecake since we got here."

Mark responded by vigorously licking the pie tin clean.

"That's not right, man."

"Nothing's right," replied Mark sullenly, throwing the pie tin to the table and startling Timmy's wife and children. They had been nearby, working on a small fruit salad, blissfully unaware of Mark's existential breakdown, as they were neither telepathic nor understood human languages. The squirrels looked around skittishly. Once they were certain there were no more pie tins being thrown, they resumed their meal.

Mark raised his hand and indicated to the waitress to bring another cheesecake.

"You can't think like that," pleaded Timmy. "It's not healthy."

"I can be however I want!"

Prior to the cheesecakes, Mark had also ingested a decent-sized bottle of whiskey.

"Is it the hotel or the vending machine?" requested Alexa Kostopoulos, sitting opposite Mark, although not directly opposite, because then she would have been hit with the pie tin. "Because we can get you a new one of either."

"What's the point?" With a heavy sigh Mark sunk lower into his seat. "There is no point. It's all pointless. Broken and dull and unable to be written with."

The former hotel owner leaned forward and placed his forehead on the Formica table.

The great and majestic city of Secaucus, in what was formerly the state of New Jersey, was still the metropolitan hub of the northeastern section of the continent, and was one of only a dozen or so remaining in the world. Calamity after earth-shattering calamity, the resilient urban center of Secaucus thrived, remaining a place of business and culture and a surprisingly low murder rate.

The Plaza at the Meadows, the shopping center that had housed the former Secaucus Holiday Inn, however, was having a harder time of things than the rest of the city. Firstly, the plaza had been built in the center of a swamp that regularly smelled of the decaying corpses of urine-soaked sewer denizens, despite being mostly corpse-free. Secondly, there had been a number of fires a couple of years earlier, started by an anonymous blonde man of Scandinavian descent, that destroyed all the competing hotels in the shopping center. Allegedly and theoretically, the arson spree was committed as an effort to drive tourists away from the other smoking husks of hotels and to the relative safety and more-or-less clean beds of the Holiday Inn. In practice, though, the fires served only to scare tourists and travelers away from the entire plaza, as they all assumed it was only a matter of time before the arsonist came back to finish the job and incinerate them in their sleep.

Things didn't get any better for the Plaza at the Meadows after that. Every year that passed brought more apocalypses and fewer members of humanity left breathing. Between the frequent ghost pirate raids, the zombie frogs, the racist alligators, and the Burger King, word got out that the Plaza at the Meadows was not as desirable as the many alternative commercial centers within the sprawling boundaries of mighty Secaucus. The final nail in the coffin was the outbreak of flesh-eating chlamydia in the plaza's only remaining office building. There were no survivors.

With no office, there were no office workers, and with no office workers, there were no customers for the remaining shops. They began to close one by one: the deli, the Chili's, the cocaine bazaar. All gone within the span of six months.

Mark Hughes was not taking it well.

Mark hurled the empty pie tin across the diner like a Frisbee.

"Sir," said the waitress, ducking out of the way, "please stop doing that."

"Why the hell should I?" slurred the former hotel owner.

"It's dangerous and stupid and it means I have to do more work later."

"That's not my problem."

The waitress looked at Mark with lowered eyes, her ocular implant whirring and turning a deep, unsettling red.

"I will make it your problem, sir."

"Hey," said Mark, sliding toward the edge of the booth, his own ocular implant clicking impotently in return, "I have a pneumatic penis. What do you say we take it for a spin?"

The waitress threw him through the diner window.

CHAPTER FOURTEEN:
BREAKING NEWS

"THIS IS SAM STONESTREET FOR WWOR with the six eighteen news.

"We begin tonight with continuing coverage of the massive power outage that has blighted the land. As society prepares to enter the second month of this godforsaken blackout, we can, at least, take some small comfort in the fact that the Cannibal Season seems to have ended, presumably because someone somewhere finally remembered that there are other animals and foods that can be consumed, foods that don't have thumbs and own houses and scream at you from a barricaded bathroom every time you try to make a sandwich from a small child's thigh.

"Moving now to our top story this evening, the complete and total failure of our electrical infrastructure appears to have spread to the sun, as even the outdoors has now been plunged into a deep and even more unexpected onslaught of total darkness, complete with dropping temperatures and falling ash, and we are all going to die in a new ice age. This, of course, is only an extrapolation of what I can see from the studio's windows, but one has to assume the view from this dismal, despairing industrial waterfront is exactly the same as everywhere else on the planet.

"After leafing through WWOR's library of mildewed and out-of-date reference books, this reporter feels comfortable presupposing there has been a supervolcanic eruption in, let's say Chile, because that's the only place this book mentions that I know for a fact still exists and that I can find on a map.

"Apparently, claims the book, this permanent night is probably the result of an explosion of nearly three thousand megatons, or three times the size of the atomic bomb those fundamentalist merpeople accidentally detonated under the Pacific Ocean exactly one year ago today, maybe, depending on what day today is. Enough crap has most likely been thrown into the sky to blanket our planet for years, obscuring the sun entirely and plunging Earth into a volcanic winter the likes of which we have never seen.

"We here at WWOR realize this news is of little comfort, but I would much rather make a guess at the specifics of this heretofore unconfirmed catastrophe than simply shrug off this nightmare as yet another vague, undefined way the world is trying to kill me.

"This has been Sam Stonestreet for WWOR. Please be sure to join me again at six twenty-five when I'll update you on our earlier story about talking to yourself in front of a fleet of non-functioning cameras in a futile effort to stay sane because you've been living in an abandoned news studio for weeks, drinking your own urine and eating old transcripts."

CHAPTER FIFTEEN: SUPER SIZE ME

SOMEWHERE NEAR THE GOLDEN ARCHES of St. McLouis[11], the bright orange sky began to suddenly and disjointedly get dark. And not the abnormal kind of deep purple dark that everyone was used to. This was a sinister kind of dark, thick and grey and ashy and blocking out any and all light the sun feebly hurled against it.

Queen Victoria XXX stopped the tank on an overpass next to the archway. The passengers sat in the yellow glow of the curved neon, staring off over the jagged cityscape, watching the crawling blackness envelop the horizon. The nearer and thicker the darkness got, the harsher and brighter the Arches glowed. Eventually, the grey sky began to fall on them in ashy chunks.

"That can't be good," said Chester A. Arthur XVII.

"What is it?" asked Queen Victoria XXX.

"I don't know. I feel like I should, like the answer's on the tip of my brain's tongue, but that doesn't even make sense."

"I'm telling you this now as a courtesy: If you keep getting stupider I will break up with you."

"That's only fair," replied Chester A. Arthur XVII. "Can you at least try to withhold judgment until after we meet with a scientist who specializes in people and not robots?"

"I make no promises."

The grey flecks began to collect on the windshield. Queen Victoria XXX turned on the wipers. The temperature plummeted like a coyote off a cliff.

"Can you turn on the heat?" asked Catrina, pulling her long, hooded cardigan tighter.

"Oh, I'll turn on the heat," said Thor, thunder rumbling in the distance.

"Is that you," began Queen Victoria XXX, "or the –"

A brilliantly white bolt of electricity slammed into downtown St. McLouis, tearing through the black cover of ash and igniting the debris-filled sky. The roiling firestorm spread outward for miles.

"Holy nuts," said Boudica IX, leaning against the window and peering upwards. The other passengers – except Chester A. Arthur XVII – did the same.

"You know you probably just killed some people, right?" Ali offered.

"Hey, so, those weren't normal clouds," said Thor, studying the crackling red and black atmosphere.

"You just set the *sky on fire*, Thor," said Catrina.

"Verily."

"It can't be any worse than whatever else was going on up there," said Chester A. Arthur XVII, staring as best he could through the windshield.

"I beg to differ," said Queen Victoria XXX.

A trio of smoking ducks crashed onto the hood of the tank.

"What the hell was that?" asked Catrina.

"Do you think they're edible?" suggested Boudica IX.

CHAPTER SIXTEEN:
NATURE FINDS A WAY

MARK, TIMMY, AND TIMMY'S FAMILY had been crashing above the Olympia IV grill and bar, in Alexa Kostopoulos's apartment, for several days. The apartment was tiny, very blue, and constantly smelled of lamb, but it was the closest thing they had to a home at the moment.

Alexa didn't seem to mind cooking and caring for the displaced cyborg and his squirrel friends. Whether this was because the extra occupants provided additional body heat and meant a smaller fire in her trash can and therefore less chance of Alexa burning her apartment down, or because the Greek woman was physically incapable of cooking for fewer than ten people, she hadn't specified.

Despite Timmy's affirmations and protestations, Mark had spent most of his time either drunk or sleeping, and was in fact currently both of those things on Alexa's couch. The super-squirrel, meanwhile, was trying to explain to his wife and four children that they couldn't go outside because they were not adequately prepared in either size or coat thickness to deal with a volcanic winter and, as a result, they would probably freeze to death and freezing to death was not good. Every time he thought they understood, one of them would scamper up the wall and began clawing at the windowpane.

It was at that moment, with Timmy retrieving one of his children from the window, that several members of PUTA – People for the Unethical Treatment of Animals – kicked down the apartment door and barged into the tiny blue living room. Turning their respective heads spastically, searching the corners of the room, the group found the squirrel family and began creeping towards them.

"We heard there were a group of squirrels here being treated with respect and dignity," hissed the closest one, his back hunched and his eyes bulging.

"You should all be ashamed!" snarled another.

"Animal lovers!" barked a third.

The cacophony of voices roused Mark from his slumber long enough for him to attempt to get up from the couch. He promptly fell to the floor, landing mainly on his face, and passed out again. A rotund female from the back of the pack waddled over and dumped a bucket of lead-based paint onto the drunk man's back anyway.

She rejoined the rest of the PUTA members, who had by now cornered the squirrels, arranging themselves in a semicircle around the tiny creatures, laughing and staring and hurling epithets. Standing on his hind legs and facing the intruders, Timmy spread his arms and pushed his family behind him. He fixed his tiny face with the steeliest gaze he could muster.

"If a single one of you cocksuckers hurts them," he threatened, "I swear I will —"

The squirrel was immediately tasered.

Here is a brief highlight reel of the things that had happened to Timmy the super-squirrel in the last eighteen months:

- he was kidnapped, experimented on by a team of scientists, and inadvertently given telepathic and telekinetic powers, at which point he murdered the scientists in question with his brain

- he was thrown into a low orbit around Earth by an angry Aztec snake-god, a snake-god who was quickly beaten to death by the reborn Norse God of Thunder

- he was attacked by an elderly mad scientist with a penchant for electromagnetic weaponry and lost his telekinetic abilities, forcing him to scratch the old man's face off the old-fashioned way

- he fought off an invasion of ghost pirates, all of whom were either dematerialized or ran away screaming

Here is an even briefer list of the points that should be taken from this:

- Timmy had very strange reactions to getting electrocuted
- things did not end well for people that attacked Timmy

The shortest trespasser opened his dolphin-skin knapsack, handing out several heavy knives and rusted hammers, before throwing Timmy's unconscious, twitching body unceremoniously into the bag. The PUTA people circled closer around Timmy's wife and kids, wearing unsettling smiles and waving knives and smacking hammers into their palms. The squirrels huddled together, shrinking back and pressing against the wall. The youngest rodent began frantically scratching at a floorboard hoping to dig his way out.

The People for the Unethical Treatment of Animals reached down toward the squirrels, blades and hammerheads first.

Then they levitated two feet in the air.

The knapsack drifted gently to the ground.

"What the hell?" asked all of them, to one degree or another, the swear words and inflection varying somewhat from member to member.

The animal-hating dickhead with the taser was flipped upside down and slammed into the hardwood floor several times before he knew what was going on. He found himself hovering eight inches from the ground and staring face-to-face with a very pissed off Timmy.

"You guys picked the wrong squirrel to fuck with."

The animal-hating dickhead with the taser was removed from his skin.

CHAPTER SEVENTEEN:
OPPENHEIMER IS GOING TO BE PISSED

HARRY HARTCOX, OWNER AND SOLE employee of Harry's Homemade Atomic Energy and Appliance Repair, a ramshackle service station and junkyard off a disused interstate in the flats of what used to be Kansas, hefted his jury-rigged fission reactor into the back of his battered pickup and prepared for the morning's delivery. The reactor, slowly being rocked farther into the truck bed, looked remarkably like a front-loading industrial clothes dryer, largely because it was a front-loading industrial clothes dryer, albeit with most of its insides rejiggered. The machine hummed idly, a slight glow coming through the circular front window, as Harry pulled the straps tight around it.

Harry was alternately proud and ashamed of this particular nuclear fission reactor, the same as he had been for the last few before it. The blackout had been a saving grace for his business — before the solar storm he had very few customers, situated as he was squarely in the middle of nowhere. His acres of uranium and scavenged home appliances and spare reactor parts lay in piles around the reclaimed service station he called his home, serving no purpose other than to keep the blowing dust from getting into his windows.

Now, though, between the electrical grid failure and the volcanic winter, Harry had so many orders lined up that even if he never got another one, he'd be able to retire comfortably for seventeen lifetimes. The problem, of course, was that he was quickly running out of supplies. Hence the clothes dryer. Harry knew it wasn't the safest, that the lead shielding was superficial at best, and quite frankly it was ugly and well below his normal standards. But he also knew it worked and that it would give some desperate family a source of heat and electricity for as long as they needed it.

Unfortunately for Harry, though, mere moments after he started the pickup and moved the gearshift out of park, the fission reactor strapped into the truck bed erupted with a terrific explosion, sublimating Harry, his truck, his home, and the two giant elk nearby — one of whom had flipped the truck and one of whom had run headlong into the clothes dryer, nullifying every one of its safety mechanisms and setting off the gigantic mushroom cloud that currently hung in the air.

Harry Hartcox was dead before he knew what happened. The giant elk were dead two weeks before they even knew who Harry Hartcox was. Yet they stood complacently in the nuclear blast, their bodies being washed away molecule by molecule, leaving only the ghosts of the old women known as "Typhoid" Mary Mallon and Lizbeth "Lizzie" Borden.

"Goodness," said Mary, staring up at the massive cloud blotting out the already blotted out sky. "That was quite the explosion."

"You have articulated my sentiments precisely, Mary," replied Lizbeth. "I do hope we get to make more of them."

"Indeed, yes. The list the gentleman gave us has at least half a dozen more nuclear emporiums of one sort or another. I imagine they will all go up in similarly spectacular fashion."

"Oh, that is such wonderful news."

"I dare say it is, my dear Lizzie."

"Please tell me that the others are in more populous areas?"

"I cannot say that I know for certain, darling, but I do suppose we will find out soon enough!"

"Typhoid" Mary Mallon and Lizbeth "Lizzie" Borden chuckled with glee, the tremendous winds from the fission detonation still blowing sand and ash through their ethereal frames. The ghosts hovered there a few moments more, watching the mushroom cloud slowly dissipate.

"That was ever so delightful!" cried Lizbeth.

"It truly was," said Mary.

"Can we go to another hydroelectric plant next?" Lizbeth begged giddily. "I did so love the way the last proprietor gurgled as we held him beneath the water."

"All in good time, my dear, all in good time."

CHAPTER EIGHTEEN:
THE BOY WHO CRIED WEINER

"I SPY WITH MY LITTLE EYE," began Thor Odinson, former Norse God of Thunder, "something that begins with C."

"Is it bigger than a breadbox?" asked Ali Şahin absently, gazing out the car window at nothing in particular.

"No. I mean, I don't think so. What's a breadbox?"

"Is it something real this time?" Catrina rubbed her forehead. "Not something you made up with your eyes closed?"

"Yes."

"Is it edible?" asked a fully invested Boudica IX.

"Sometimes."

"Is it one solid color?"

"Yeah, most of the time."

"This game is so stupid," grumbled Queen Victoria XXX.

"You just hate it because you're a terrible guesser," said Thor. He meant the statement as an insult to his friend and her poor attitude toward time-honored road trip games, but had, instead, inadvertently stumbled onto the truth. Queen Victoria XXX *was* a terrible guesser and had always hated games that involved such. Road trip after road trip after road trip she would fail at them. The replicated royal lowered her eyes and floored the accelerator.

"I'll give you guys a hint," continued Thor. "It's long, narrow, and rounded at the tip."

"Are you staring at your dick again?" barked Catrina, turning and glaring at the thunder god.

"No. I said it begins with a C."

"OK, fine, are you staring at your cock again?"

"No," said Thor. "Look, I've been staring at it for the last hour, at least."

It was Ali's turn to spin in his seat and glare at the thunder god. "Are you staring at Catrina's tits again?"

Catrina reached over and smacked Thor across the face.

"'Tits' doesn't begin with a C!" he shouted, rubbing his cheek.

"My cans then, you fucking asshole," snapped Catrina.

"I wasn't staring at your tits!"

"Was it just her nipple then?" asked Boudica IX.

"It's nobody's nipple!" Thor blurted out. "Odin's earwax. You're all wearing heavy sweaters."

The redheaded queen looked down at the bulky cable knit sweater covering her breasts.

"Oh, right."

Catrina growled anyway and turned back around, sliding low in her seat and crossing her arms, and her thick cardigan, tightly over her chest.

"That was a pretty fun game after all," said Queen Victoria XXX, smirking into the rearview mirror.

"You're only saying that 'cause your boobs are up there," grumbled the hotel clerk.

"I was looking at corn!" Thor finally admitted. "Corn! We've been driving through nothing but cornfields for the last two hours. What is wrong with you people?"

"I said corn," said Chester A. Arthur XVII.

"You didn't say anything," corrected Ali.

"Uh-oh," said Catrina.

In the distance, far beyond the frosted fields of cornstalks, a mushroom-shaped cloud unfolded against the darkened horizon. A fast-moving wave of cereal grass soon crashed across the landscape, the sea of cornstalks bending, breaking, and flying toward the custom-built tank. The vehicle shook slightly as the blizzard of corn slammed against it.

"It's OK," said Chester A Arthur XVII calmly, "the car's insulated against radiation."

"We know," said Catrina and Thor simultaneously, unconsciously matching their levels of exasperation with the dead president's repeated reassurances.

"That is the third one today," said Queen Victoria XXX, squinting out the window at the fading cloud. "What the hell is going on out there?"

CHAPTER NINETEEN:
PLEASE DON'T SUE ME, DISNEY

THE LITTLE MERMAID SAT ON THE frigid beach, basking in the sunshine despite there being no sunshine to bask in, waves gently lapping at her fins. She was small and beautiful, a thin line of seaweed wrapped around her large breasts, a smile on her face. The fishwoman methodically ran a butter knife through her golden hair while she hummed contentedly to herself, seeming not to have a care in the world.

"Excuse me," said a man with a voice like gravel, strolling across the shoreline, "I don't mean to intrude, but I've a favor to ask of you and your kinfolk."

The mermaid turned toward the man, her head tilted.

"What's a intrude?"

"To bother," the man translated slowly. "I don't mean to bother you."

"What's a you?"

The man in the wrinkled suit narrowed his eyes slightly.

"What's your name, dear?"

"Deer?" said the mermaid, twisting around excitedly. "Where?"

"You'll have to excuse her," said another mermaid, altogether more formidable, riding a crashing wave and slipping deftly onto the shore, "she took an outboard motor to the head a while back. She hasn't been the same since."

"What's a since?"

"I see," said the man.

"Ooh! Bunny!" The blonde mermaid began flopping down the beach, chasing after a terrified crab.

"What's this favor you were talking about?" asked the second mermaid. Her entire torso was wrapped tightly in seaweed, from her armpits to her fins. She had broad, flat shoulders, and her short hair was pulled back strictly. This was a creature built for swimming.

"Are you aware of the hydroelectric plant a few miles out from here?"

"Of course."

"Well, if it isn't too much trouble," said the man, with all the charm of a veteran car salesman, "I'd like for you to go ahead and dismantle it. Cripple the entire platform, kill the crew, and bury it beneath the ocean."

"Why in the Marianas Trench would we do that?" countered the mermaid, crossing her arms over her chest. "Aside from the fact that Aquamatica is extraordinarily kind and cooperative to our people, and overlooking the fact that they employ a third of the mermaids in this oceanic quadrant, crashing the plant would do nothing but pollute our own realm."

"You mean you don't know?"

"Don't know what?"

"About the... I seem to have forgotten the correct term. Tremendous hazard, plaguing the mermaids..." the man said, pouring honey over the unpaved road of his voice. "Please remind me of what to call it."

"The carcinogenic sludge?"

"Yes! That's it, thank you. I can never remember the word 'carcinogenic.'" The man bowed slightly. "The sludge is being produced by Aquamatica."

"That's impossible."

"I'm afraid it's true."

"But the sludge is coming from the east. Aquamatica is to the southwest."

"Well, they're not fools now, are they?" explained the man. "They've been transporting it east and dumping it into the ocean, moving their illicit disposal far enough away that the mermaids would never suspect them."

"You're lying," said the mermaid unsteadily.

"What would I possibly have to gain by lying about this?"

The mermaid glared at the grey-haired man in the suit, connecting what she knew to be true with what the man was saying.

"If you'll bear with me," he continued. "The sludge, does it appear to be some matter of factory run-off? Man-made, to the best of your assumptions?"

"As best as we can guess..."

"And, other than Aquamatica, what other industrial production facilities are in this immediate vicinity?"

"Only Amalgamated Envirorapist, up the shore a few miles."

"But if it was Amalgamated Envirorapist, surely the lauded minds of the mermaids would have been able to discern that."

"We have investigated them a few times," said the mermaid, her defenses lowering, "and we've never been able to pin it on them."

"That really only leaves the one choice, doesn't it?"

"Yeah, I guess. Look, I'm just not sure —"

"I understand completely," said the man, really drowning the pebbles in his throat with all the sweetener he could find. "I'm but a single voice, and a land dweller at that. But I beg of you to please at least pass the word along. Investigate the hydroelectric plant for yourselves. I'd hate to think the great race of the mermaids was continuing to suffer needlessly."

"I'll let our environmental investigators know," said the mermaid, turning slightly and sizing up the wrinkled, salt-and-peppered man over her shoulder.

"Please do," said the man. "And I hope you'll keep in mind that Aquamatica's complete and total destruction is going to be your best defense against future harm."

CHAPTER TWENTY: ORIGIN STORY

MARK HUGHES SAT AT THE WINDOW, staring sullenly across the snow and ash-covered expanse of the Plaza at the Meadows to the scorched, skeletal remains of the Secaucus Holiday Inn. Timmy the super-squirrel sat on the windowsill at his side, telekinetically manipulating a needle and turning an old pastel-striped hand towel into a cape. The rodent's family rested in a pile of shredded packing paper in a large wooden salad bowl on the table behind them. From a room on the far side of the tiny apartment came the sounds of Alexa Kostopoulos wrecking her toilet.

"Mark," thought the squirrel, "we've got to get out of here."

"She ate some bad fish," explained the human, still gazing absently out the window, his forehead resting on the cold glass. "We all did."

"Not that," replied Timmy, his tiny stomach gurgling slightly with the reminder. "I'm talking about you; you keep staring out the window. It's not healthy. Your hotel's not coming back."

"I know."

"And neither is peanut butter. But if all I did was hang around thinking about it all day you wouldn't hesitate to yell at me."

"I know."

"Then knock off the morose sitting on your ass all the time, boss! We can wait till you OD on sadness and I lock you in a bedroom for two days if you want, but that seems like a shitty idea to me."

"When you put it like that, sure." Mark shifted, finally turning toward the squirrel.

"Look, Alexa's great and all, but this isn't what we do," continued Timmy. "You and I don't sit around waiting for stuff to happen. I'm genetically predisposed to sleep for six months out of the year and *I'm* getting antsy."

"What are we supposed to do?" Mark demanded. "I put years of effort into making sure that hotel stayed standing and it all disappeared in an afternoon. Starting over now seems exhausting, whether it's another hotel or a motel or a hostel or whatever. One earthquake or tyrannosaur in heat and it could all be over."

"I'm not talking about investing in some new thing, Mark," said Timmy. "I'm talking about investing in yourself."

The squirrel put down the needle and draped his new cape over his furry shoulders.

"Join me," he said, extending a tiny paw. "Together we can fix this piece of shit planet."

Mark stared at the cape-wearing rodent incredulously. A draft from the window caught the cape and began ruffling it majestically.

"You're serious?"

"I'm serious."

"What about your family?"

"They'll be fine with Alexa. She takes care of them better than I ever did. My wife, my kids... They've never understood my powers, my responsibility. And they'd be in more danger with me than without." The tiny squirrel waved a paw dismissively. "Think of whatever comic book movie you want and pretend I'm giving that speech."

"Does that mean I'm the sexy reporter?"

"You're the old, black cop."

"The one who's getting too old for this shit?"

"Yeah."

"I thought you said this was a comic book movie."

"Look, I don't actually watch a lot of movies, OK?"

"It's really cold out there," said Mark, staring toward the endless dark clouds of the volcanic winter again.

"Well, sure," thought Timmy out loud, "but once you grow a pair you should be fine."

"All right, I'm in," said Mark, a smirk inching his mouth upward. "But I'm not wearing a cape."

A slight gurgling sounded from their stomachs, building into something significantly less slight. From across the apartment came a loud crack, as of porcelain breaking. Alexa Kostopoulos yelped.

"Maybe we give it a day or two to get this fish out of our system?" groaned Mark.

"Yes," said Timmy, bolting across the apartment toward the kitchen sink.

CHAPTER TWENTY-ONE:
GETTING THE BAND BACK TOGETHER

THE GOD, THE GIRL, THE CLONES, and the cybernetic donut maker arrived at Dr. Arahami's volcano lair, El Mal Muerte, in the middle of an artificial forest in the middle of a very real desert in the territory of Las Máquinas[12]. The sky hung low overhead, still black and terrifying, but no longer on fire, so there was less threat of choking to death on combusting oxygen, which was always good.

The sextet stood huddled together at the base of the jagged, dormant igneous mountain, snow falling heavily around them. Catrina was bouncing from foot to foot, her long cardigan pulled as tight as the fabric would allow. This did little to nothing for the section of her legs between her ruffled skirt and her boots, though, as they were clad only in thin tights.

"I'm beginning to rethink ever listening to you and your 'don't wear pants when you're saving the world' speech," said the tiny Filipina woman, bouncing up against Queen Victoria XXX.

"If they start making women's pants that don't require twenty minutes and bottle of baby oil to squeeze into, I'll reconsider," said the dark-haired queen. She pulled the ragged slit of her layered dress up slightly, revealing a handgun and several knives holstered to her thigh. "Besides, I like having access to my arsenal."

"That doesn't help me at all."

"I never told you to get a skirt that short."

"I think it's bracing," said Boudica IX in her even shorter skirt.

"Yes, but that's because you're insane," said Ali, shivering in his sweatshirt and cargo pants, his good arm crossed over his chest. "It's maybe twenty degrees out. We're all freezing. Except for Charlie and his stupid vintage wool suit."

"It's actually less helpful than you would think," replied the president, laying on his back in two inches of snow and ash, the melting precipitation soaking into his pants and jacket.

"Remind me never to take any of you to Jötunheimr[13]. Or Finland," said Thor with a dismissive shake of his head. He knocked on the colossal metal door before them.

"Dr. Arahami?" asked the thunder god, looking around and hoping to find the hidden security camera. He knocked again.

"What if he doesn't have any generators?" suggested Queen Victoria XXX.

"He has generators," answered Ali.

"What if they don't work?" countered the queen.

The Norseman knocked again. There was no response.

"We're going to have to find a way in," said Chester A. Arthur XVII from where he lay in the slushy cinders. He spit a falling flake of ash from his mouth.

Thor knocked again, much, much harder. The giant door shuddered and fell inwards.

"Done," said the thunder god.

***

"Lee?" called Chester A. Arthur XVII, slung across Thor's shoulders. "You here?"

The group wandered through room after room of utter darkness, occasionally bumping into furniture or bouncing off the edge of a doorway. Eventually they found the roboticist in his kitchen. Dr. Lee Arahami was sprawled on the tiled floor, his shoulders slumped against his cabinets. A few stumps of candles flickered from the countertop. In their wavering glow, the six visitors could see dried blood on the doctor's chin and a belt wrapped around his thigh as a tourniquet.

"Lee?"

The doctor stirred, his eyes blinking in the dim light.

"Charlie?"

"Lee, what the hell happened?"

Thor placed the inert, sopping wet body of Chester A. Arthur XVII on the floor next to the scientist.

"The power went out... and... I couldn't leave. The door... it wouldn't open. I had to... I had to eat my own foot," explained the doctor. "I taste terrible."

"Duck?" asked Boudica IX, pulling an electrifried wing from her bag and holding it out to the scientist. "It's a little cold."

The doctor's eyes widened. He shifted slightly on the floor, his shoulders twitching. He moved his head forward with notable resolve but nothing else followed.

"Would you mind feeding it to me?" he inquired, falling back against the cabinets. "I don't seem to have the strength necessary to move my hands."

***

One lightning strike to the volcano lair's high-volume capacitor, one to Chester A. Arthur XVII, one to a passing trio of coyotes, and several handfuls of painkillers later, the scientist and the sextet of homeless road trippers convened in the plush lounge just to the left of the heart of the volcano. A spread of gamey canine meat was laid out on the coffee table in the center of the room, wholesale-sized containers of salt, pepper, and tabasco sauce resting between the steaming legs and inconsequential ribs.

"So can you help us?" asked Chester A. Arthur XVII, sitting on the arm of the sofa.

"Of course," said Dr. Lee Arahami, leaning back into a purple, highly-piled armchair. He bit into another coyote thigh, holding a paper plate beneath his chin. "I was going to go and repair the grid myself but the generators died and I got trapped here before I could finish researching the issue. Assuming nothing's happened to the drones I sent out, I should have a full list of the materials that failed and need to be replaced in another few days."

The roboticist's footless leg dangled just above the carpet, teeth marks still visible on the ragged, gangrenous stump. He reached down to scratch the wound.

Catrina Dalisay, visibly disturbed by the act, said, "Don't you need medical assistance for that?" She was sitting cross-legged on the floor, nearly at eye level with the scabbed limb.

"This?" replied Dr. Arahami, raising the septic appendage into the air. "I'm just going to cut it off at the knee and replace the whole damn leg."

"And when exactly are you planning on doing that?"

"Before we leave, at the latest."

"Shouldn't that be, you know, a higher priority?"

The doctor shrugged. "If it gets infected, it gets infected."

"What do you mean 'if?'" asked Ali Şahin, tilting his head and staring at the rotting wound. Something green and thick dripped from it and fell to the rug.

"Hey, speaking of unnecessary surgery," interjected Queen Victoria XXX, "how do we un-robot Charlie? I'm sick of hauling his useless ass all over the place."

"Hey," said Chester A. Arthur XVII.

"*You're* sick of it," grumbled Thor Odinson.

"What are you guys talking about?" asked the roboticist.

"You may have missed it in your half-starved delirium," began the cloned president, "but I wasn't functioning properly, or really at all, when we arrived. By my calculations, I've got about eighteen hours left before I start shutting down again. And that's only as long as I don't do anything strenuous."

"Which is complete bullshit," added Queen Victoria XXX.

"My best guess is that the solar storm shorted out all the subdermal transformers powering my cybernetic implants," continued Chester A. Arthur XVII. "Thor's been recharging my capacitors, but it doesn't last very long and every time I get hit with lightning part of my brain dies."

"Is that what's happening to the redhead too?" inquired the doctor, pointing his half-finished coyote leg at Boudica IX. She had dressed a number of bones up in some of the less burnt fur and was playing with them in the corner, dancing them around like dolls and talking to herself.

"No, that's just Bo," said Queen Victoria XXX.

"Are you sure?"

"Yeah," said Thor.

"Huh."

"Can you fix Charlie or not?" demanded Queen Victoria XXX.

"Do you want me to fix him or 'un-robot' him? Because those are two very different things."

"The second one."

"You're sure? Remove his cybernetic implants and replace them will all that soft, squishy meat that died so easily last time?"

"Yes," replied the queen. "I'm actually very fond of the soft, squishy meat."

"Heh. You said soft, squishy meat." Thor chuckled.

"Then, no, I can't help you," continued Dr. Arahami, shaking his head and ignoring the thunder god completely. "What do I look like, a rogue biologist?"

"Yes?" suggested Thor.

"Do you know one?" asked Chester A. Arthur XVII.

"Of course," replied the scientist.

CHAPTER TWENTY-TWO:
A MIDSUMMER NIGHT'S KEGGER

CHRYSANTHEMUM STAGGERED THROUGH the immense forest of evergreens, as quickly as the seventeen shots of ambrosia in his system would allow, stopping only twice to dig his overly enthusiastic thong out from between his glittering green ass cheeks. And also once to pee. And then once to ask directions from a deer. But that was it.

Eventually the wood nymph made his way to the Fraternal Lounge of the Woodfolk[14], located deep within the bowels of the forest, somewhere near the sphincter of the woods. The lounge was situated in a large clearing in the densest cluster of trees, protected from the global volcanic winter by the thickly knit branches and lit by mutant fireflies. Despite the serenity of the setting, the scene was one of utter chaos and debauchery, as it often was. Casks upon casks of ambrosia littered the grassy field, an overturned goat was on fire, and passed out dryads with penises drawn on their foreheads lay slackjawed against logs. On the far side of the clearing a beer pong game had turned violent and bets were now being taken on the probability of the ensuing bodily injuries. Everywhere else was a video store back room's worth of gleaming green genitalia and bouncing breasts and butts, the result of no fewer than three simultaneous orgies.

"Guys. Guys!" shouted Chrysanthemum, leaning against a tree at the edge of the lounge and trying desperately not to vomit. "I just ran into this old guy, out near the old interstate, and he was all like, 'Excuse me? Are you a wood nymph?' like he was trying to sell me a mattress or something, so I was like, 'What of it, old man?' and he goes, 'I need you and your brethren to destroy Pan's Pan-Recyclables,' and I was all like, 'Why?' and he says, "Cause,' and then I was like, 'OK.'"

"What?" asked Moonbeam, currently situated between, and not stopping what she was doing with, Cactus Flower, Pigweed, and Delilah.

"He was an old guy, in a shitty suit, and he said he worked for someone or something, maybe the government? And he said something about Pan's doing something we don't like. I don't... I don't really remember what."

Hemlock, an enormously muscular, moss-covered nymph wearing the tiniest banana hammock ever, shrugged and said, "I've heard of flimsier excuses to tear shit up." He hurled an empty cask into a tree for absolutely no reason.

"WHO'S UP FOR A RIOT?!" he bellowed.

Every free hand in the woodfolk lounge shot into the air with an enormous cheer.

"Hot damn," said Hemlock, punching a nearby dryad across the face and shattering his teeth. "Let's go cause some problems!"

There was another chorus of cheers, followed by a symphony of X-rated moans, followed by several of the wood nymphs vomiting on their feet.

CHAPTER TWENTY-THREE:
SHE WAS A BIG FAN OF GEORGIA O'KEEFFE

"IS THIS THE RIGHT VOLCANO?" asked Queen Victoria XXX, gazing up the sheer igneous wall before her, and then at the sheer igneous wall above that. The reddish-brown volcano loomed nearly a quarter-mile over the foursome, the blunted rectangular peak nearly fluorescent against the backdrop of dark clouds of ash. The luxury-tank sat idling behind the group, casting its headlights through the falling snow and into the distance.

"They never put out signs or mailboxes or anything," grumbled Thor. "Should I knock?"

"Can we skip to the breaking in?" suggested Boudica IX. "I'm finally getting cold."

"Yeah, all right," replied Chester A. Arthur XVII with what would have been a shrug had his withdrawing electrical circuits been capable of it. "Lee's life was electronics and he couldn't handle the blackout. I'm pretty sure this biologist is just going to be another corpse."

"Maybe she's in the shower," said Thor.

"Open the door, Thor."

"OK," replied the Norseman with a shrug.

Thor grabbed the door handle and, with only slight wrenching and buckling, slid the solid steel plate open.

"Hello?" he said into the darkness that greeted him. "Scientist lady?"

"Dr. Gonzalez?" asked Chester A. Arthur XVII, limping forward. "Joselin?"

"I don't think —"

Several dozen thick, thorned vines shot out from the darkness and wrapped themselves around the foursome, lifting the trespassers several feet into the air.

"Son of a bitch," said Queen Victoria XXX, thrashing several feet above the ground, reaching for one of the knives strapped to her thigh.

"I fucking hate plants," growled Thor, flexing his arms slightly and tearing through the vines like they were significantly overcooked spaghetti.

Crashing to the ground, Thor began freeing Boudica IX from the thorned tendrils, only to be tackled by an enormous black batflower. Seriously, enormous. This thing was at least twenty feet tall. And that wasn't even counting the massive earthenware flowerpot that dragged behind the plant, dredging a gulley into the slushy ground. Extending from the ceramic planter was a long black stalk, weaving upward until it burst into a mane of dark purple leaves. Sprouting from the center of the leaves were several dozen thin tendrils and a number of nearly-black pitcher flowers that appeared to be lined with teeth. Because they don't give out mad scientist designations for not giving plants teeth.

"Holy crap," said basically everyone.

The dark tendrils coiled themselves around Thor's extremities and pinned him to the ground. He struggled beneath them, but they were proving to be much stronger than pasta. The black batflower leaned forward, lowering its flower-mouths toward the thunder god. Rows and rows of wet teeth glistened in the headlights of Chester A. Arthur XVII's tank.

"Why are you mad at me, plant?" shouted Thor. "I haven't eaten a vegetable on purpose in years!"

The largest of the pitcher flowers engulfed the Norseman's head and shoulders. The rest of the group heard a muffled cry of "This is disgusting!" before even darker clouds rolled in, leaving them dangling in almost total blackness.

There was a rumbling in the heavens, then a bolt of lightning came streaking down, crashing into an empty patch of dirt halfway between Thor and his friends and lighting up the volcano like the interior of a strip club at closing time.

"Twenty feet north, Thor!" shouted Chester A. Arthur XVII.

"Which way is north?!" muttered Thor through the plant. Another bolt of lightning hit the ground, dangerously close to Queen Victoria XXX.

"The other way!" she shouted. "Other way!"

On the opposite side of the thunder god, a lone tree was illuminated and then erupted into flames.

"Too far!" shouted Boudica IX.

"Fuck it!" barked Thor. Then he struck himself with lightning.

The black batflower reeled, the pitcher that had been gnawing on Thor's skull reduced to cinders. The tendrils unspooled from the thunder god, springing back toward the center of the plant and attempting to put out the small fires that were smoldering along the edges of its petals. The plant begin rolling in the dirt, attempting to smother them.

Thor sat up and shook his bleeding head.

"That was weird."

"What the fuck are you doing to my plants?" shouted a voice.

The god and the clones turned to look – or attempted to look, as half of them were still being held at strange angles and squeezed by thorned vines – at the figure striding from the volcano. The curvy Latina appeared to be wrapped in a thick bathrobe and carrying an unmounted machine gun at her hip, her white lab coat thrown over the robe and flapping in the breeze behind her. Her sopping wet hair fell from the half-done bun on her head, spilling over her face and shoulders. Red-tinged sunlight spread outward from her, as the clouds above appeared to be burning away.

"Are you Joselin Gonzalez?" inquired Chester A. Arthur XVII, currently being held upside down and above the scientist.

"Yes," replied the biologist. "How do you know my name?"

"Lee Arahami sent us."

"Also your name tag is on your lab coat," said Boudica IX, splayed awkwardly and hanging by an ankle.

"Oh, right," said Dr. Joselin Gonzalez. "Why were you trying to break into my volcano?"

"We thought you were in trouble," said Chester A. Arthur XVII, "because of the blackout. We found Lee half-dead in his kitchen."

"I was taking a shower."

"I fucking told you!" shouted the perforated thunder god.

"What do you want?"

"I would like to have my cybernetic parts replaced with normal flesh and blood parts," stated Chester A. Arthur XVII.

"Make sure you fix his dick," added Queen Victoria XXX, examining the multitude of scratches she received freeing herself from the vines.

"And I would like a couple Band-Aids," said Thor, raising his hand, his face resembling a Jackson Pollock painting.

"You guys have money?" the scientist asked.

"Yes," replied the dead president.

"And an unending supply of free electricity," said Queen Victoria XXX, pointing a thumb toward Thor.

"Also, I set the sky on fire again and we're probably all going to choke on burning ash clouds if you don't let us in," added the thunder god.

"Doesn't your car have a ventilation system?" countered the biologist, nodding toward the idling tank parked fifty feet away.

"Well, yeah," countered Thor, "but it's all the way over there."

The doctor shrugged and said, "All right, what the hell. Come on in."

The vines released their grip on the president and the Celt and they were unceremoniously dropped to the ground.

CHAPTER TWENTY-FOUR:
MILE HIGH CLUB

DR. ARAHAMI'S COLD FUSION-POWERED industrial hovercart, running on a pre-programmed autopilot, whisked across the never-ending ashtray of desert, churning up clouds of snow, soot, and sand in its wake. Ali Şahin and Catrina Dalisay had enthusiastically offered to run an errand for Dr. Arahami, retrieving three dozen ultra-voltage macro-transformers, the first of the supplies needed to repair the continental grid, from the abandoned scientific stronghold of Los Alamos. The couple had literally jumped at the opportunity, and then sprinted out the door, eager for any opportunity to get some alone time away from their increasingly unwashed friends.

Near the front of the elongated hovercart, Catrina hugged herself tightly, somewhere within the seams of the oversized parka she had borrowed from the mad roboticist. Her top half was actually quite comfortable in there, but her bottom half was still only wearing a skirt and tights, and the weather was going out of its way to make her regret that choice.

"I thought deserts were supposed to be warm," she muttered.

"Sometimes they are, but sometimes they're extraordinarily cold, especially at night. Or during whatever the hell this is," explained Ali, looking up at the blanket of clouds smothering the atmosphere. "On normal days, there's little to nothing to trap the ambient heat. Meaning if the sun's not out, it gets cold fast. And if the sun's been forcibly removed from the equation for whatever reason, you might as well burn all your t-shirts. For warmth. So you don't freeze to death."

"That's dumb."

"That's nature."

"Nature's dumb."

"Nature's *angry*, and it hates us," said Ali. "Of course none of that explains why Arahami didn't put any heaters in this thing."

"Maybe he hates us too."

The temperature rapidly dropped another few degrees and the couple began shivering. Ali pulled his hood up awkwardly with one hand. Catrina squatted down into a wind-free corner of the hovercart and pulled her knees into her parka.

"Did you learn all that desert stuff from your encyclopses, or whatever you called them?" she asked. "Those weird giant books you talk about sometimes."

"No. I grew up out here, a few hours north of Los Alamos, in what used to be Colorado," explained Ali, kneeling next to Catrina and rubbing one of her arms. "Our desert was a little different, though. During the Community College Wars, all the sand was melted into glass. Just an endless ocean of it. Got hot as hell when the sun was out, and it was always out."

"And you lived there on purpose?"

"Hey, so there's another fun fact about the deserts out here," he continued, sitting down and wrapping his one functioning arm around his girlfriend. "They're all a mile above sea level."

"Is that so?" replied Catrina, leaning into him. She craned her neck to kiss him.

CHAPTER TWENTY-FIVE:
TRUTH OR... MORE TRUTH, I GUESS

CHESTER A. ARTHUR XVII SAT STRAPPED into a surgical chair, connected to a number of beeping, blinking machines. His skullcap had been removed and was lounging in a bin at his side.

"How do you have power?" he inquired. "Did your solar panels survive the mass ejection? And then ignore the eternal night?"

"No, I lost all solar inputs during the geomagnetic storm," replied Dr. Joselin Gonzalez, standing over him and poking at his brain with assorted tools of varying pointiness. "Thankfully I had already devoted an entire sub-basement to composting, using the output of the anaerobic bacteria to fuel a number of backup generators. And of course there's all the chimps in the basement hooked up to electroencephalographs. I can run most of the day-to-day operations off their brains' electrical activity alone."

"You're not kidding about that are you."

"I am not."

"Huh," said Chester A. Arthur XVII. "Is there a lot of upkeep?"

"Not really. They crap right into the compost sub-basement."

"You are by far the maddest scientist I have ever met. And I'm friends with a guy who gave me a jackhammer for genitalia."

"Thank you," said Dr. Gonzalez, blushing. "Lee's a good guy, but he's really more pathologically obsessed than 'mad.' He doesn't even have any henchmen."

"Neither do you, though," said the aerated president, knitting his brow — or at least the portion of it that was left attached to him.

The mad neurologist clicked her tongue twice and a walking nightmare tottered around the chair and into view of Chester A. Arthur XVII. From the neck down Dr. Gonzalez's sidekick was a koala, adorable and cuddly and wearing a tiny white lab coat, but that all stopped at the head. Instead of a face there was a mass of octopus stinkhorn — a large, fleshy fungus that erupted into a cat's cradle of curled, red tentacles upon maturity. The fungus arms twitched and coiled wanly with every breath the creature took.

"Holy shit."

"I know, right?"

***

Queen Victoria XXX rested her arm across the wooden back of a thinly-padded, brightly-striped sofa. She was staring vaguely across a sitting room that appeared to have been furnished entirely by IKEA as some kind of promotional stunt. This was, of course, impossible, as all IKEAs were burned down during the Torrent Wars[15], but the resemblance was uncanny.

"I'm torn," she said. "On the one hand, she's giving me Charlie back the way I prefer him, non-electrical and slightly less likely to injure me if I accidentally hit him while we're sleeping. On the other, she and Charlie can talk about all his science bullshit without translation and that threatens me in the tiniest way, not because she's smarter than me, but because she gives a shit. I both want to hug this doctor bitch and hit her, and part of me wants to sleep with her because God *damn* those breasts."

"I would sleep with you or her or anyone with a vagina," said Thor, sitting beside her on the couch and hunched over the cocktail table. "And the vagina isn't actually the sticking point I make it out to be."

"I am well aware of that and that is precisely why I do not and cannot take you seriously and why I have a hard time understanding why Boudica is with you. Your lack of standards make her appear to have no standards. And, her spontaneous anarchic episodes aside, she seems lovely and like she could do better."

"That was hurtful, but I understand completely."

"What is wrong with you two?" asked Boudica IX. She was sitting on the floor on the far side of the coffee table staring at them with mild horror.

"I think there's something in this vodka," said Thor, lifting a clear glass bottle from the tabletop. Boudica IX took the bottle and gulped down a mouthful of the liquid.

"It's not vodka," she said, "it's refined sodium thiopental with..." The Celtic queen ran her tongue over her teeth. "... methylphenidate."

"Neither one of us knows what that means," said Queen Victoria XXX.

"Truth serum and Ritalin."

"Oh fuck," barked the cloned Victorian royal.

"Who the hell just leaves that laying around their refrigerator in an unmarked bottle?" barked Thor.

"Why were you drinking unmarked liquids, dummy?" replied Boudica IX.

"Because I'm not very smart and I really wanted a drink and even though I thought it might have been some kind of poison I didn't really care if it was and I died because I still haven't entirely gotten over being stranded here on Midgard with all you insignificant mortals! Sure, getting my powers back helped, and most of you seem nice enough, especially you, Bo, but I really want to go back home!" shouted Thor. He stood and then he screamed indiscriminately. "Odin's sparsely shaven scrotum, make it stop!"

"You and your father are too close!" shouted Queen Victoria XXX, rising and pointing at Thor.

"Thousands of years of reverence and nigh-omnipotence were yanked out from underneath me! My father is the only one who understands that and is actually willing to talk to me! All the other gods I've been able to find hate me!"

"That's because you're very arrogant! You need to work on your personality! And your hygiene! When you sweat you smell like a locker room toilet!"

"I am well aware of that!"

"This is awesome," said the wild-haired warrior queen, bouncing up and down where she sat. "Hey, Vicky, how often do you poop?"

"Every other day! I don't get enough fiber!"

"Do you pick your nose?"

"Ferociously!"

"How much do you love Charlie?"

"More than I will ever adequately be able to describe! There aren't words in the entirety of all the world's languages to express my feelings for him, and I suck at music and I think art is dumb! Sometimes I lie awake at night worried that he doesn't truly know how much I care for him, but I've never been able to tell him because my feelings for him are so deep and eternal and ridiculous that I am literally physically paralyzed any time I stop and dwell on it with anything more than a glancing thought!"

"Holy crap."

Queen Victoria XXX screamed and slammed the bottom of her fists against the wall. She fell to the couch, sobbing.

"I love him so god damned much."

"I think you crossed a line," said Thor, "although I'm not really sure what line. Catrina just told me it's bad to make a woman cry and when you do it's crossing a line."

"It's OK," sputtered Queen Victoria XXX. "She's not the one making me cry, it's these stupid *feelings*."

"Speaking of Catrina," said Boudica IX, narrowing her eyes and looking at Thor, "if she and I were both about to get mauled by a pack of rabid yeti, who would you save first?"

"Catrina," said the thunder god with heavy resignation. "Although if it was only the one pack of rabid yeti, I'd go ahead and save you both."

"How did you beat all of us in Scrabble that one time?"

"I roofied your coffees."

"Why wouldn't you let me move into your hotel room?"

"You fart in your sleep. A lot."

"It smells and sounds like you shit your pants," added Queen Victoria XXX.

"Those lacy pink underpants in your dresser," continued the redhead, unabated, "did you really buy them by accident?"

"No." The fallen deity spoke through gritted teeth. "I saw them and I kind of wanted to know what they felt like and so I tried them on and they made me feel even prettier than usual *and* they were on sale, so I bought them and I wore them a bunch and they are my favorite underpants."

"Who would win in a fight," yelped Boudica IX, "Bruce Lee or Robocop?"

"Robocop," Thor answered begrudgingly.

"Superman or Batman?"

The thunder god clenched his fists and bit down on his lower lip. With every ounce of the near-limitless strength he had, Thor fought the urge to answer. But the sodium thiopental was vehement and he had put away a lot of it. Finally, he blurted out:

"Superman! Are you happy?! Superman would win in a fight against Batman! It wouldn't even be close!"

The Norseman punched a massive hole into the wall, then slumped against the wood paneling and slid to the floor.

"Why are you doing this to us?" he asked, near tears, his head hanging between his knees.

"An abundance of curiosity and a lack of empathy, mostly," replied Boudica IX. "I'm gonna go see if there's any popcorn in the kitchenette. Does anybody want anything?"

"Charlie," sniffed Queen Victoria XXX, laying across the couch and burying her head under several pillows.

"For you to forget I said something bad about Batman," said a dead-eyed Thor.

"I meant, like, a soda or something."

CHAPTER TWENTY-SIX:
ONE OF THE CLASSIC BLUNDERS

AFTER THE FIRST ROBOT WAR ENDED the world for the ninth time, Los Alamos, in what was then the state of New Mexico, was rechristened as the capital of the United States of America, its scientists ruling as democratically-elected kings and queens. Billions of dollars were funneled into technological research and, in short order, cancer was cured, global warming was reversed, and electric cars became commercially viable and less ridiculous-looking. Everything – literally, everything – that scientists had spent years toiling over and hypothesizing about, hamstrung by shoestring budgets and time-travelers from the eighteenth century using the Bible as legal precedent, became a reality.

Los Alamos rose shimmering into the stratosphere, a soaring, glittering cityscape of chrome skyscrapers, high-speed monorails, and no fewer than two Thunderdomes.

Catrina and Ali stood in front of an unmarked warehouse, several dozen nearly identical warehouses surrounding them, the plain of storage centers dwarfed on all sides by shining towers of abandoned architecture. Knee-deep in filthy snow, the couple sized up the large retractable door of slatted aluminum before them. Hunching down and each grabbing a handle, the hotel clerk and the donut maker, with an enormous heave and some small grunting, threw the door open.

The door slid upward with remarkable ease, despite being almost a hundred feet long, rattling up and then back and disappearing into the interior of the warehouse. The grey daylight of the volcanic winter flooded weakly into the pitch blackness inside, an overflowing toilet of dirty sunshine. Ali and Catrina could just make out tower after tower of stacked electrical equipment, the smallest components the size of compact sedans.

"Are these the transformers?"

"Why does nobody label anything here?"

When the Kingdom of Los Alamos was deposed – the former rulers chased out of their city by heavily-armed helicopters – the scientists did what they had to do to survive. Some took jobs with private companies, some with the government's new Department of the Biggest Gosh Darned Explosion You Ever Saw. Most, though, retreated to the surrounding volcanoes and underground laboratories littered across New Mexico, waiting and plotting, stewing in their resentments until they boiled over and became full-fledged supervillains and mad scientists.

Still standing in the gaping maw of the building, Catrina and Ali examined the warehouse before them suspiciously, looking in corners and near the rails of the door for motion sensors or laser cannons or any other signifier of an alarm system. Not finding anything, the couple looked at one another and then tentatively took a step inside.

Lights flickered on overhead. The donut maker and the former hotel employee instinctively ducked. Looking around and realizing they hadn't exploded, Ali and Catrina unfolded and headed onward.

"If anything moves," began Ali, walking slowly forward, "run away. Run away screaming if you can so that I can hear you and run away too."

"This isn't the first mad scientist's supply closet I've broken into, babe."

This was, in fact, the sixth warehouse that Ali and Catrina had found a way into. Each and every one had been unmarked and unlocked, but heavily fortified in some other terrifying way once they got inside. There had so far been man-eating raccoons, nuclear spiders, two powders that were almost certainly poison, confused and elderly armed guards, and several roadrunners the size of professional basketball players. Catrina and Ali had survived them all with aplomb, despite several close calls and a large number of scrapes and scratches.

The lack of any kind of horrible defense system on this most recent warehouse, however, they found particularly unnerving.

Upon leaving, all the former kings and queens made a gentleperson's agreement to leave Los Alamos as it was, a veritable candyland of expensive equipment and technological resources. They had built themselves a utopia of reason and science and they would continue to take advantage of that achievement for as long as they could.

An email was sent around and the scientists vowed to use the resources of Los Alamos wisely and efficiently, taking only what they needed when they needed it.

Catrina hopped from the forklift, limping toward Ali. She found her boyfriend staring with head aslant at a green-marbled bowling ball hidden between two sets of now vacant shelving.

"Why are you staring at a bowling ball?" she asked.

"Why is there a bowling ball in a warehouse full of transformers?"

The tiny Filipina woman tapped a boot against the ball, spinning it slightly. She quickly pulled her foot away.

"Why does that bowling ball have a clock?"

"Why is the clock counting down?"

"Odin's stanky toenails."

"We should probably run. Away. Screaming."

Which isn't to say anyone actually made it easy to do that.

CHAPTER TWENTY-SEVEN:
I AM THE NIGHT

MARK HUGHES AND TIMMY THE SUPER-SQUIRREL crouched atop the roof of the ancient apartment building, staring out over the crisscrossing streets of downtown Secaucus. From behind the hovering comforter of dark grey ash, a bright orange moon could only barely be seen, brilliant lunar light banging furiously on the cloud cover and screaming to be let in.

The former hotel owner waited patiently along the edge of the building, vaguely silhouetted by the infinitesimal glow of the grey-orange moonlight. There he knelt, watching, brooding, a gargoyle made of meat and a large faux fur-lined snowsuit. His squirrel friend waited, watched, and brooded beside him, his cape fluttering dramatically.

"Er ee oong es ite?" queried Mark, turning his head toward the rodent.

"What?" replied Timmy, scrunching his tiny brow. "You told me not to read your mind without permission. What are you saying? Why are you wearing that mask?"

"It's cold," explained Mark, pulling down his fleece face mask. "And I don't have a thick layer of fur to protect me like some animals I know."

"That sounds like a personal problem to me."

"Are we doing this right? We've been up here for hours and we haven't seen a god damned thing. We haven't even seen a person who could do a thing."

"You have to give it time, chief."

"I'm about to give it all my extremities. I can't feel my fingers or my toes. I think this new ice age is really shitting in our crime-fighting cereal."

"Ice age seems strong," replied the squirrel.

The cyborg pointed across the street to another building. Each and every window was frozen over; icicles the size of evergreens dangled from the building's eaves.

"I still think you're being a little hyperbolic."

"I think it's time to pack it in, buddy."

The super-powered rodent sighed.

"We're going to have to go somewhere else," said Timmy, shaking his whiskered head, "somewhere where the criminal element isn't such a bunch of shriveled wangs. Somewhere more terrible. Somewhere horrible. A desolate, blighted place, where morals have been kneecapped and left for dead, and people will do anything for a dollar, regardless of the frozen wasteland outside. Somewhere like Detroit. Or that island infested by Kardashians."

"Well, we're not walking," countered Mark, slipping his mask back on. "Em eesing I owls eff."

CHAPTER TWENTY-EIGHT:
ANY SUFFICIENTLY ADVANCED
TECHNOLOGY...

A KOALA WITH THE HEAD OF AN ACID TRIP rushed into the sitting room of Dr. Joselin Gonzalez's volcano lair and began hopping up and down, gesticulating wildly.

"What the hell is that?" said Queen Victoria XXX, a look of disgust sprinting across her face.

"I don't know and therefore I think I should step on it," said Thor Odinson, manfully wiping away tears after his girlfriend's latest round of serum-induced interrogation. The thunder god moved toward the creature. Boudica IX held up her hand.

"I think he works here," explained the Celtic leader slowly. "If I'm understanding correctly, and I think I am, Joselin sent him. He's saying, 'The doctor needs the blonde guy who craps lightning.' Is that right, little guy?"

The little guy shook his plant head vigorously, the curled fungus bouncing up and down and shaking loose a small cloud of pollen.

"Please don't do that again," said Thor, waving the dusty spores away from his face. "I'm getting less and less respectful of Bo and her wishes and I can't guarantee that I won't squish you next time you bother me, just so I can bother her."

"Ooh," said Boudica IX, a slight chill running through her. "I like it when you threaten harmless little animals."

The thunder god raised his eyebrows. Then, looking at the mad scientist's henchthing, he cocked his head and said, "Things aren't looking good for you, little guy."

The koala with an abstract sculpture for a head backed out of the room slowly.

"I take it back," said Queen Victoria XXX. "You're not too good for Thor, Bo."

***

"He's crashing," said Dr. Joselin Gonzalez, motioning toward the motionless figure of Chester A. Arthur XVII, "and my defibrillator just shit the bed. Can you zap him back into something resembling life?"

"Not if you want this room to stay standing," said Thor.

"What?"

"I don't make thunder," he explained, "I call it down from the heavens. I'm not some kind of weather balloon."

"That's scientifically impossible," replied the neurobiologist. "You're clearly an anomaly of some kind, capable of manipulating nearby electromagnetic spectrums to your will. Also that's not how weather balloons work."

"*I'm* scientifically impossible. That's kind of my whole deal."

"Your friend is in several barely connected pieces right now and we're not going to be able to get him out of this room without him losing at least one of those parts permanently," she said.

"As long as it's his left arm, he'll be fine. He barely uses the thing."

Dr. Gonzalez exhaled and rubbed her eyes with the palms of her hands. Then she said, "Do me a favor, Thor. Close your eyes and pretend that 'the heavens' are, I don't know, six inches above your head."

"Uh, OK, sure."

"You there? You picturing it? Wherever it is that you do your thing from, right above your head?"

"Yep."

"OK, good," she said. "Now bring the thunder."

"Are you –"

"Don't think, Thor, just do it."

"OK."

Thor's brow furrowed slightly and a thin, dark cloud materialized across the operating room, stretching from wall to wall and obscuring the overhead florescent lighting. The faintest rumble of thunder echoed from all corners. A bolt of light the size of a baseball bat seared the air between the thin cloud and the exposed cerebellum of Chester A. Arthur XVII.

Thor opened his eyes just in time to see Chester A. Arthur XVII gasp back into consciousness. Around them a number of small screens and devices were sparking and resetting.

"Well I'll be damned," said the thunder god. "I would have bet donuts to more donuts that was going to kill you both."

"Congratulations," said the doctor. "You're not magic after all."

"I don't think that's the lesson here."

"Did I just die again?" asked Chester A. Arthur XVII, staring at the large blonde man who hadn't been there seconds earlier.

"Only for a couple minutes," Dr. Gonzalez stated. "It's kind of standard when you're Frankensteining someone into a new body."

"Frankensteining?" said Thor, suddenly interested in his friend's rehabilitation. "Is he going to have giant, ropy stitches and neck bolts?"

"Don't be stupid," said the mad scientist. "I'm a professional."

"What about patches of different colored skin?"

"It depends on who I have in the freezer."

"Can you give him bear arms?"

"You can go now, Thor."

"I'm actually OK with bear arms," said Chester A. Arthur XVII.

"No you're not," replied Dr. Gonzalez. "I left a scalpel in your neocortex."

CHAPTER TWENTY-NINE: ANIMAL FARM

DOZENS UPON DOZENS OF FARM animals ran from the barn as an enormous foot crashed into the structure. Behind the fleeing horses and cows and pigs, a decomposing space lizard, the size of a large office building, roared and stomped the barn into the slushy ground.

"All right, Lizzie. Your point has been made," said the ghost of "Typhoid" Mary Mallon, standing with her ethereal arms crossed as the last of the livestock stampeded past. "We can possess the corpses of extraterrestrial reptiles. I was wrong."

"That is all I wanted to hear," replied Lizbeth "Lizzie" Borden from within the deceased husk of scales and spikes. She dispossessed the space lizard and let the rotting corpse crash to the snowy ground

"That was quite the show of excess, my dear. I had my comeuppance the moment you forced that beast to lumber up from his shallow grave. You did not need to assault the barn as well."

"My hatred of horses is unparalleled, Mary. You are well aware of that."

"Then why did you kill only three?"

"Because terror is a finer punishment than death. Those asinine equines will now be scarred for the rest of their hopefully short lives. The horses will live in fear of space lizards forevermore."

"Everything already lives with that fear, Lizzie, all the time."

"Yes, but horses are notoriously slow-witted and now they have something visceral to draw from."

"If you say so, darling," Mary acquiesced, shaking her head. "Now come on, we have dillydallied enough here. There are energy concerns that need ending."

"That richly-dressed man is not paying us, Mary. We are receiving no recompense for assisting him," explained Lizbeth. "He simply requested that we tailor our cross-country killing spree toward the businesses and hobbyists on his list. We are not indebted to him in any way."

"I am aware. But we gave the man our word, and I shall not go back on a promise. Besides, I do not get as much glee from terrorizing livestock as you do. I find it somewhat juvenile, if you would care for my honest opinion. I much prefer the maiming and murder of actual humans."

"You are no fun sometimes, Mary."

CHAPTER THIRTY:
THE TWILIGHT BARK
WON'T SAVE THEM THIS TIME

THE GREY-HAIRED MAN IN THE thrift store suit was en route to a convention of mercenary deconstruction workers when he saw it: a small, square building, churning out an almost endless stream of exhaust and surrounded by several whirring turbines. A dozen electrical lines stretched from the rotor apparatus to a factory off in the grey, slushy distance. The man in the suit pulled his red Hummer off the main road and drove the vehicle straight through the ice-covered chain link fence surrounding the structure. Neither the smaller building nor the factory was on his list of known energy concerns, but the man wasn't about to take any chances.

Shoving open the door – marked Property of C.D.'s Fine Furs – the man strode onto the latticed power station floor, high on his own indignation. He stopped almost immediately. At least a hundred filthy, rusting cages lined the walls of the building; in each one was a small dalmatian, a running wheel, and a dangling dog biscuit. Frayed, sparking wires ran along the walls, connecting the cages to the turbines outside.

The dogs scampered in the wheels frantically, incessantly, nearly perpetually. Should one of the dogs stop, either to pant or poop or because it tripped, a howler monkey walked over to the cage and smacked the dalmatian in the head with a newspaper until it started running again. If the dog didn't run fast enough, the monkey lit a cigarette and then put it out in the puppy's hindquarters.

"Holy shit," said the man in the suit.

"Can I help you?" crawled a low voice sounding of cigarettes and tranquilizers.

"I don't think so," replied the man in his own unpaved timbre. He turned toward the voice and found himself face-to-face with an ancient crone in a nightgown made of extra sheer snakeskin. She exhaled a mouthful of mentholated smoke into his leathery face.

"Then I would politely ask you to leave."

"In a moment," he said, putting up a hand. The man turned to look at the dogs again, then back to the woman. He shook his head in admiring disbelief.

"I'll be honest with you. I came into this establishment with every intention of convincing you to burn your own building to the ground. I work for a concerned party looking to get a monopoly on the energy supply to this continent and your self-sufficient electrical generators caused me some alarm. But, quite frankly, after coming in here and witnessing this puppy mill firsthand, I feel strangely compelled to leave you and your customers alone."

"Customers don't concern me," drawled the woman. "All the electricity generated here is carried directly to my coat factory. The coats are made from the slower puppies."

"You are a truly depraved individual."

"That is what I'm told."

"What are you doing for dinner this evening?"

CHAPTER THIRTY-ONE:
NO WORSE FOR WEAR

THIRTY-SIX HOURS AFTER THEY STARTED, Dr. Joselin Gonzalez and a newly re-humanized Chester A. Arthur XVII emerged from her operating room into a small white waiting room. The cloned president was almost entirely covered in gauze and neon self-adhering bandages – as well as some small spots of paper towels and masking tape – and still a little gimpy, limping heavily and clutching his side as he exited. He inched forward, his brightly-wrapped feet shuffling over the linoleum.

Turning his unaltered head and neck stiffly from one side of the room to the other, the re-re-reconstituted politician found nothing but empty taupe chairs.

Queen Victoria XXX, perhaps the most appreciative of this miracle of science, was not there to witness the momentous event, as she and Thor, the sodium thiopental still not entirely out of their systems, had locked themselves in the doctor's library, lest they accidentally be honest with someone. Boudica IX, bored with knocking on the library door and shouting invasive personal questions at her friends, was taking a nap on the sofa in the sitting room.

"I was expecting more fanfare," said Chester A. Arthur XVII.

"It's really not that big a deal," said Dr. Gonzalez. "Sometimes I do this twice a week."

"It's a big deal to *me*."

"OK, Charlie, OK," replied the doctor, patting him on his neon green shoulder with a practiced mix of consolation and condescension.

In the other room, Boudica IX shifted on the couch and farted loudly.

***

Meanwhile, at the other volcano lair, Catrina Dalisay and Ali Şahin returned looking not particularly dissimilar from shit, their hovercart loaded down with industrial transformers and dredging a deep valley across the glacial desert. Snow and ash were falling heavily all around them.

"Why do you two look like the worst part of a bad burrito?" asked Dr. Lee Arahami, sporting a new, shiny leg and meeting them at the loading gate in the rear of the volcano. "I gave you guys the easy task."

"There was a bomb, Lee," Ali explained slowly, rigidly stepping from the hovercart. "Some kind of singularity. Engulfed the entire warehouse and then just collapsed into nothing."

"OK, sure."

"Before that there were raccoons, a powder that blinded me for several hours, gigantic radioactive spiders."

"So many spiders..." added Catrina softly, her face empty of anything.

"Oh, the booby traps," said the scientist. "I didn't tell you guys about them earlier?"

"They bit us, Lee," said Ali.

"Everywhere..." Catrina whimpered.

"The raccoons or the spiders?"

"Then, as we were leaving, we triggered some kind of perimeter defense," continued the donut merchant, his eyes vacantly staring past the scientist. "We drove through a wall of fire that burned our parkas, and most of our eyebrows, clean off. We had to drive back without them, without coats. Through a snowstorm. In a hovercraft without heat."

"It was so cold..."

"So we decided to cover ourselves in mud for insulation... We had to dig through a foot of snow to find it."

Ali fixed his gaze on Dr. Arahami. Catrina shuddered violently, remembering what happened next.

"There were scorpions in that snow, Lee. Giant fucking scorpions.

"We had to fight them off," he continued. "I lost a shoe. And most of the leg it was attached to."

Ali pulled up his ragged, sopping pants leg, revealing a makeshift tourniquet and harness binding a large, broken pincer to his bloodied calf. His leg fit almost perfectly into the concavity of the cracked claw. His balance was impeccable.

"And then," said the brown-skinned man, his voice dropping the better part of an octave, "then it started to get windy."

"Why couldn't you have just added heaters to the fucking hover-carts?!" screamed Catrina, emotion suddenly flooding back to her. Emotion that was mostly seething rage.

"I'm sorry. I didn't think it was necessary," said Dr. Arahami, staring at Ali's leg with clinical detachment. "It doesn't get cold out here."

"Yes, it does!" shouted Ali, rushing to the doctor and grabbing him by his lab coat with his good hand. He pressed the scientist against the frame of the loading gate. "You've lived out here for years, Lee! You know that's a god damned lie! DESERTS GET COLD!"

"At night, sure," stammered the doctor. "But who goes out at night?"

Ali released the roboticist and began stamping awkwardly around in a circle, swinging his arms spastically and mumbling incoherently. His girlfriend joined him.

"I'll unload the transformers myself," said the scientist. "You two go take a shower, have some hot chocolate. Calm down a little."

"I'm going to do the first two, and probably at the same time," said Catrina, fixing the doctor with a stare that would have turned coal into diamonds and then melted them, "but I make no promises on the third."

The couple stomped across the receiving area toward the stronghold of the mad scientist, trailing muddy foot- and clawprints behind them.

"Can you guys wipe your feet before you –"

"Fuck you!" was the stereophonic reply. Multiple middle fingers were raised.

CHAPTER THIRTY-TWO:
THE DOCTOR HAD AN EXCLAMATION POINT OVER HIS HEAD

SEVERAL HOURS LATER, AFTER A LONG and therapeutic shower that used up most of Dr. Arahami's hot water, Catrina and Ali made their way to the lounge. They found their friends returned from the other mad scientist's volcano lair, the "How exactly are we fixing the world?" meeting already in progress. Dr. Arahami was hunched over the coffee table, a map and an indecipherable notepad laid out before him. Queen Victoria XXX and Chester A. Arthur XVII stood on either side of him, while Thor and Boudica IX sprawled on the couch opposite the trio.

Ali and Catrina, still slightly soggy, flopped down into the empty purple armchair in a tangle of legs and odd angles.

"Can't you just use your right hand?" Queen Victoria XXX was asking.

"That's what she said," added Thor.

"No," continued Dr. Arahami, unabated. "The fasteners are extraordinarily thin and purposely made to be fragile. You have to be delicate when you're screwing."

"That's also what she said."

"What the hell are you guys talking about?" asked Catrina.

"Left-handed spork-head screwdrivers," explained the exasperated roboticist. "I need one to swap out several processors and about a half dozen cables in the regulator units. The spork-heads were custom made for the APSCAM government, so no civilians could go around messing with government equipment. Any other tool – and even the right tool misused – will shatter the screws. Only a few manufacturers were licensed to make them, and only one of those manufacturers made them left-handed, a lefty boutique in Fisherman's Wharf."

"Fisherman's Wharf, San Francisco? Where all the souvenir stores and chocolate shops were?" asked Ali.

"Exactly," replied the doctor. "APSCAM had a habit of hiding things in plain sight. They didn't think too highly of the people that voted them into office."

"Wasn't San Francisco burnt to —"

"What *else* do we need?" demanded Chester A. Arthur XVII abruptly, standing with arms of varying thickness and pigmentation crossed over his lopsided chest. The reconstructed president was still crusty and a little smelly-looking thanks to Ali and Catrina's monopoly on the shower. "We've been on this damn screwdriver for nearly ten minutes."

"I think I liked the old new you better, Charlie," said Catrina.

"Joselin fixed the leader-y part of his brain and he's not used to having that stick back up his ass yet," said Queen Victoria XXX. "Plus he's been mostly dead all day and I think it made him cranky."

"I think one of these new body parts has a nicotine addiction," added the president. "I haven't wanted a cigarette this bad in years."

"Well, too bad. I hate it when you smoke."

Chester A. Arthur XVII grumbled, Queen Victoria XXX glared, and then Dr. Arahami continued.

"We'll need twenty pounds of isotonium to rebuild the bus distributors at the substations," said the scientist. "Most of them spiked and depleted when the transformers overloaded. The closest mines I could find were in the southwestern quadrant of the Irish Colombia territory. Unless my intelligence is incorrect you won't be able to go more than ten feet without tripping over a lode."

"I don't like how you qualified that," said Queen Victoria XXX.

"You said 'lode,'" added Thor with a giggle.

"The last and most important item we're going to need is a trivection cooling unit. Without it, the perpetual motion engine running the generators will overheat and we'll be worse off than when we started," said Dr. Arahami. "The only unit I was able to track down is owned by a despotic madman with an industrial machinery fetish."

"Tyrone Tainthammer, the Earl of New London?" suggested Thor.

"Yeah, that's the guy," replied the doctor. "How did —"

"Tainthammer?" queried Queen Victoria XXX.

"He used to be a porn star," explained Thor.

"You guys are making shit up now, right?" asked Catrina. "You went over the real plan before we got here?"

"I really hope not. I've always wanted to meet Tyrone Tainthammer."

"Sorry, Thor, but that's not happening," explained Dr. Arahami, "you have to come with me. I'm going to need you there to help me move the heavier pieces around and jump start the perpetual motion engine."

"Where is 'there' exactly?" inquired Catrina.

"The main electrical grid for the North American continent is Montana," answered Chester A. Arthur XVII.

"In Montana, you mean."

"No. Montana. The entire state."

After an, quite frankly, inevitable uprising of sentient kangaroos in Australia accidentally led to a global chemical war that ended the world for the twenty-second time, Canada, Mexico, and the United States merged into one gigantic hyper-country, if only so that the next time a world war broke out they would each have two fewer opponents with which to contend, in much the same way a man might convert to Mormonism and marry his mistresses so that they and his wife will stop running into one another and causing scenes in his favorite restaurant.

In an effort to make their jobs easier, the government of the Amalgamated Provinces and States of Canada, America, and Mexico condensed their many disparate electrical infrastructures into one, paving Montana in its entirety and filling it in with electrical equipment, in much the same way a man might convince his multiple wives to all share the same bed with him so that he doesn't have to remember whose room he was supposed to go to on which night or worry about which key goes into which keyhole.

This actually worked spectacularly well, right up until the Amalgamated Provinces and States of Canada, America, and Mexico exploded due to incompetence, in much the same way a man with multiple wives is incredibly happy right up until they simultaneously divorce him when it becomes apparent that he's a dickhead.

Post-solar storm, however, and with no government to maintain it, the state-spanning electrical grid was no longer doing anything except sitting there, rusting and slowly leaking coolant from a variety of cracks, in much the same way a septuply-divorced man beaten by a bouncer with a pool cue sprawls face downward in a dark alley, gurgling in a pool of his own fluids.

"Which one has the lowest chance of death?" asked Ali.

"Do you mean short-term or long-term?"

"That is a terrible answer."

"I call dibs on the screwdriver!" yelped Boudica IX.

"Once everyone has everything," said Dr. Arahami, "meet me and Thor in the primary control room of Montana. It's the biggest of the five buildings on the grid and has a giant neon sign on its roof that you can see for miles. You can't miss it. If everything goes as planned we'll have gone across the grid and replaced everything by the time you get there."

"If there's nothing else," said Chester A. Arthur XVII, "I'd suggest we get going now, before we waste any more time. People are freezing to death out there."

"I have to pee," said Boudica IX.

"Me too," said Thor.

"I kinda do too," said Queen Victoria XXX.

"OK, fine, bathroom breaks for everyone," said the cloned president. "*Then* we get going."

"No, you're taking a shower first," corrected the reconstituted royal. "I'm not sitting with you smelling like a hospital laundry room for another minute."

"And I need to get Lee to replace whatever it is that makes my arm work," said Ali, limply flapping his inert forearm. "I kept forgetting to ask."

"The hemo-electric turbine?" replied the doctor. "Sure."

"And there's the leg now, too." Ali waved the red-tinged stump of his heavily gauzed calf in the air, the scorpion claw duct-taped to it wiggling unsteadily.

"How come he gets to wear animal parts?" asked Boudica IX.

"OK, bathroom breaks and we fix Ali, but after that –" began Chester A. Arthur XVII.

"I'm starving," said Catrina.

"I'm also that," said Thor.

"OK, yeah, that's a good point," said the president. "I don't think I've eaten in two days."

CHAPTER THIRTY-THREE:
WE INTERRUPT YOUR REGULARLY SCHEDULED BROADCAST

"THIS IS A KARK 4 SPECIAL WEATHER REPORT. I'm Luanne Van Dörkenson filling in for meteorologist Rainn Bilthump, who was devoured by a t-rex several days ago while we were fleeing the KARK station after the dinosaurs that escaped from Cretaceous Park[16] descended on downtown Little Rock.

"From what I can tell by staring out my increasingly ice-covered windows, trapped as I am by a fast-moving snow bank that has impeded further progress and made opening the doors of the KARK SUV impossible, it would seem that Rainn was incorrect in his prediction of an 'eventual' ice age. That ice age is on us now and, if this reporter and her cameraman are any indication, we are all probably going to freeze to death on an abandoned highway, and soon.

"The only comfort we can take from this situation, judging from the theropods dropping like flies all around us anyway, is that the reign of the dinosaurs did not last for long. Presumably, a diet heavy in North Americans led to a mass outbreak of fast-acting diabetes among the terrible lizards. Or, you know, the freezing to death.

"With the murderous reptiles succumbing and hopefully going extinct again, I can only assume that the remaining human and mostly-human residents of the continent – the lights still off and everything outside our windows a dirty winter wonderland – are getting down with some good, old-fashioned fucking and starting to reclaim our place atop the food chain. I know I have, and will continue to, if only because body heat is the only thing keeping this SUV from freezing over entirely. It also doesn't hurt that watching dinosaurs collapse and die apparently gets me sexually excited and my cameraman really enjoys when I talk in my news voice, which I have been doing a lot, seeing as how it helps me detach myself from the utter hopelessness of my current situation and keeps me from screaming incoherently in impotent rage.

"This has been Luanne Van Dörkenson with a special report for KARK 4, Little Rock's only news source in this SUV. I'll be back at ten with a full report on my cameraman's sexual prowess."

CHAPTER THIRTY-FOUR:
WELL, THERE'S YOUR PROBLEM

AFTER JOYOUSLY SLAYING THEIR WAY across the gated communities of converted, ethanol-fueled missile silos previously known as Kansas; into and out of the cavernous, diesel-powered sasquatch reservation situated in the abandoned government bunker under Cheyenne Mountain; and through the expensive, organic, midget-driven energy mills of New Hollywood, the elite private city and entertainment mecca situated in the sprawling tunnels and hollows beneath what used to be Denver International Airport, "Typhoid" Mary Mallon and Lizbeth "Lizzie" Borden began to observe a change in their victims' attitudes towards their unceasing rampage.

"Lizbeth, my darling," said "Typhoid" Mary Mallon, "I cannot help but notice there have been fewer and fewer of those deliriously angry sorts stridently defending their enterprises from our fevered wrath."

"It would certainly appear to be true," replied Lizbeth "Lizzie" Borden, possessing a recently deceased rhinoceros and extricating herself from the collapsed tin shed previously known as Krazy Kurt's Khemicals and Karwash. "This Krazy Kurt fellow does not seem to mind at all that we have waylaid his alchemical initiative."

"I wonder if the man is even at home."

Mary, in the guise of a jaguar, slunk her rotting black frame through the piled snow and toward the neighboring ranch house. She put her frontmost paws up on the windowsill and peered inward.

"Oh," she said. "Oh my."

"Is something the matter?" asked Lizbeth, her rhinoceros shell suddenly foaming and melting around her, the victim of an unforeseen reaction between two chemicals from opposite sides of the tracks. She slipped her ethereal form from the rapidly decaying body and floated to Mary's side.

"I would not say that," answered Mary.

"No, I dare say everything is quite fine," echoed the ghost with a slight giggle, hovering beside the jaguar and staring intently inside the home. "Quite fine indeed."

Mary and Lizbeth continued to spy on Krazy Kurt and his wife in their firelit living room for several more minutes.

"She does seem to be enjoying herself."

"Well, you know what they say about the crazy ones," replied Lizbeth.

"Is he going to –"

"Oh my, look at that."

"They have remarkable balance."

"Is that a neighbor?"

"I do believe that is a neighbor."

"Oh my."

"She certainly is a pretty young thing," purred Mary. The jaguar began to shift awkwardly, pressing itself against the side of the house again and again.

"Mary," said Lizbeth, laughing with shock, "are you –"

"Oh, do not be so puritanical," replied Mary with mock indignance. "You cannot honestly say to me that in all your time walking this earth you have not missed those carnal desires stripped from us when we died. Or that this scene has not produced an aching in your loins."

"You might do well to note that I do not currently have any loins," explained the ghost of the elderly Lizbeth, gesturing toward the aery dress covering her phantasmal nethers.

"Perhaps then you should go and find yourself a set..." The jaguar smirked. "... and we can remedy this situation together."

Lizbeth "Lizzie" Borden clapped her see-through hands together and floated off through the volcanic winter to find a fuckable corpse.

CHAPTER THIRTY-FIVE:
THE GAME IS AFOOT, WATSON

"SO THE RV RUNS FULLY ON TRASH, RIGHT?" asked Mark Hughes, his ocular implant whirring gently[17], his arms crossed over his chest, and his telekinetic squirrel friend on his shoulder. The pair stood on the snowy lot of Easy E's RVs and ATVs in what was once central New Jersey, on the outskirts of civilized society. Before them was a sixty-year-old Winnebago, retrofitted with a deconstitution matrix, some serious off-road tires and shocks, a large plow, and a plethora of other amenities to help survive a world that had grown significantly more hostile and haphazard since the vehicle's original manufacture.

"As long as we have something to throw in there to deconstitute we'll be fine?" continued Mark. "I don't want to find out in the middle of the mutant nation that this thing actually needs gasoline."

"No gasoline, no electric, no nuclear. You have my word," replied Easy E, blinking his eyes a few times to get the sleep out of them. This was a man who believed in his products so thoroughly that he had been sleeping in one of the campers right up until the moment Mark and Timmy arrived. "You can shove your arm in there and run it off everything south of yer elbow if y' get desperate."

"Are we going to get desperate?" asked Timmy the super-squirrel. "What's the mileage?"

"Hundred to the gallon organic, seventy-five synthetic."

Mark and Timmy looked at one another, thought some things between the two of them, and nodded.

"All right, we'll take it," said Mark.

As Mark handed over the agreed-upon price of a box of homemade gyros and a case of Advil Cold & Sinus medication, a gigantic animal came tearing through the dark lot on four legs and ran crashing into the nearest recreational vehicle. The RV wobbled slightly and the beast roared at the top of what was assumed to be its lungs. It was difficult to tell for sure. The animal looked like a very large feline of some sort, a lion maybe, with paws and short fur and all that, but something about it was off. The creature immediately threw its monstrous frame ferociously into the vehicle again.

"What the fuck is that thing?" asked Timmy, his tiny eyebrows raised.

"Manticore[18], I think," said Easy E, narrowing his puffy red eyes.

Sometime after the sasquatch insurrection that followed the thirteenth end of the world, opinions toward all cryptids and creatures of legend soured significantly, and the fabled Jersey Devil[19] felt compelled to emerge from his place of hiding in the Pine Barrens of southern New Jersey and hold a press conference. A need for vengeance had overwhelmed society, and roving hunting parties – complete with balloons and cake – were often seen wandering about the streets and forests and airplane junkyards, looking for something mythical they could shoot in the face so they could feel better about themselves.

The Jersey Devil, not particularly a fan of being shot in the face, and growing tired of eviscerating hunter after hunter after hunter, came out and laid down some basic zoology and anatomy lessons, distinguishing himself from the ranks of the sasquatches and driving home the fact, once and for all, that not all creatures of fable and legend were the same. The beast spoke eloquently, and at great length, but the gist was basically, "You don't fuck with us, we won't fuck with you."

An uneasy truce settled between humanity and the cryptid world shortly thereafter, due in equal part to the impassioned speech of the Jersey Devil and the fact that if one shoots at a pack of chupacabras[20] and misses, those fuckers will swarm like a dropped beehive and start tearing off faces.

The manticore knocked the recreational vehicle onto its side, sending up a spray of ashy slush, then turned and bounded toward the trio. Timmy grabbed the leaping felid with his brain and held it in midair. The two men and the squirrel stared at the monster in awe. The creature had a body resembling that of a lion, but instead of the traditional whiskered leonine face there was a malformed human head, with row upon row of teeth, and instead of a tail there was the stinger of a scorpion growing from its hindquarters.

The mythical beast struggled and thrashed in the super-squirrel's psychokinetic grasp, mumbling under its undoubtedly foul-smelling breath.

"You ain't supposed to be here!" shouted Easy E. "We had an agreement! I ain't kicked at a leprechaun in years!"

"Things change," growled the monster.

"Change? What are you talking about?" asked Mark.

They never found out, as a harpoon burst through the terrifying face of the manticore, ending the conversation abruptly. Timmy shrugged and unceremoniously dropped the beast to the ground.

"Ho-ly shit," said a disheveled man in thermal overalls and a large flannel hat on the far side of the lot, breathing heavily and carrying an empty harpoon gun. "Di'n't think I'd catch up t' him. Gall damned thing trashed my distillery earlier. Been trackin' him all af'ernoon."

"The *manticore* trashed your distillery?" reiterated Mark, furrowing his brow. "Purposefully?"

"Sure did," said the man. "Thing came out of nowheres, wrecked up all my stills and tanks, and then took off." The dirty man snapped his fingers. "Jus' like that. Weirdes' thing is, the gall damned thing never even took a swipe at me. Hell, ne'er even a second look!"

"I don't even know you and I kinda wanna hit you," agreed Easy E.

"I know!" said the man, spreading his hands in surprise. "I get that *all the time*. Like you would not believe."

"Something doesn't make sense about all this," thought Timmy aloud.

"Yer tellin' me. All my butanol up and gone, like that!" He snapped his fingers again. "And now there's talking squirrels!"

"I'm not *talking*, chief."

"Wait, did you say butanol?" asked the former hotel owner. "The heating fuel? You've been doing well since the blackout started, I take it."

"Like a fatass pig at a pig whorehouse," said the man. "And then when it got cold to boot? Hoo-boy."

"And then it came after the deconstition campers..." continued Mark, deep in the bowels of his own mind. "Did the manticore attack anything else on the way?"

"Shoved over a few pumps in an ol' abandoned gas station off the Parkway, but that was it. Sucker ran clear through a vegetarian training camp without so much as disemboweling no one."

Mark Hughes furrowed his brow so hard that his grandkids were going to be born looking like they were deep in thought.

"Hey," said the man in the overalls quietly, nudging Easy E. "Think we can eat that thing?" He kicked at the manticore's body.

"Only one way to find out," replied the skinny man, rubbing his hands together eagerly.

CHAPTER THIRTY-SIX:
JUST BE GLAD HE WASN'T
PRAIRIE DOGGING

THOR ODINSON FIDGETED IN THE SMALLISH cab of Dr. Lee Arahami's gargantuan, overly-chromed all-terrain tractor-trailer, en route to replacing the transformers across the Montana grid. His knees hit the glove compartment and the door didn't have one of those ledges where an arm could be rested, forcing the thunder god to try to rest his elbow on the narrow lip of the window. Not surprisingly, his arm slid off more often than it didn't, and he continually bonked his head against the glass.

"You know, Charlie's tank is a lot nicer than this," said Thor, rubbing his head. "It has heated seats."

"That's great," replied the roboticist.

"Why doesn't your truck have heated seats?"

"Because I don't use it that often. It's only for transporting large pieces of equipment, and generally not very far. It seemed a little extravagant to add a bunch of amenities for something I drive once a year."

"Don't you want to be comfortable?"

"I am comfortable."

"Don't you want me to be comfortable?"

"You'll be fine if you stop thinking about it."

Thor muttered to himself, then tried to rest his arm on the window lip again. His elbow slid off again and he hit his head again, this time cracking the window slightly.

"Are we there yet?" he grumbled.

"We've been on the road for two hours, Thor," said Dr. Arahami.

"I don't know what that means."

"It means we're not there yet."

The former Norse god sighed theatrically. "When are we gonna get there?"

"Twenty hours, give or take," said the doctor with a small shrug. "A lot of it will depend on how intact the old interstates are."

"I thought you said we had a compass."

"We do," said Dr. Arahami slowly and with more than some confusion, pointing toward the antique brass compass duct-taped to the dashboard, "but that's not going to change the fact that the truck moves faster over flat, paved highway than crumbling wastelands."

"Are there any crumbling wastelands?" asked Thor, staring out the window at the blowing snow and breathtaking red cliffs flanking the road on either side. "Because so far this is pretty boring."

"Probably not. We're going west to the Grand Canyon, and then it's a straight shot north. That should keep us on some fairly preserved roads, although Idaho might be rough. The killer potatoes really did a number on them."

"Fucking potatoes."

The Great Potato Riots started shortly after McDonald's figured out a way to create french fries entirely from excess fryer grease, with no actual food involved. While a hit with discerning fast food patrons and hungover college students the world over, this slight against the venerated tater did not sit well with farmers or nutritionists.

In a tense showdown with Ronald McDonald and his army of frothing Grimaces, the potato originalists, as the farmers and dieticians had taken to calling themselves, managed to overturn an entire convoy of trucks hauling the new french fries. Unbeknownst to them, though, the recipe for the new french fries required congealing the grease with older grease for the better part of a week. As the convoy toppled to the ground, truck after truck, spilling its only half-solidified cargo, the potato originalists watched with horror as an ocean of chunky, fatty oil poured forth instead of the dreaded fake fries.

The half-congealed grease flooded across miles of the endless emerald potato fields of Idaho, seeping into the ground and waking the sleeping root vegetables from their eternal slumber.

The potatoes were not happy.

Pulling themselves from the fatted soil in a tangle of roots and excess eyes, the incensed spuds set upon those that had disturbed their rest. Within minutes, the road was nothing but a nightmare of stripped bones and engine parts. The largest of the potatoes stood atop the crumpled trailer of one of the overturned transport trucks, screaming

into the ether with cold fury and holding above it the severed head of
Ronald McDonald.

The world was doomed.

Thankfully, though, the soulless massacre didn't actually spread
much farther than the edges of Idaho before the killer potatoes began
to rot and die, slumping to the ground in wrinkly, mushy heaps. They
were, after all, only vegetables, and all vegetables go bad eventually.

"I have to pee."

"Again? You haven't even had anything to drink since last time."

"That doesn't mean I don't have to go."

"If we keep stopping we're never going to get there."

"I can pee on the floor if you want."

"What? No, that's disgusting," said Dr. Arahami. "Just go out
the window."

CHAPTER THIRTY-SEVEN:
SOME THINGS ARE HARDER THAN OTHERS

AFTER SEVERAL HOURS OF WALKING through dark, frozen scrublands; a few hours hiking through the jagged, blackened remains of an incinerated forest; one very quick, painful hour running and weaving and shoving and occasionally jump-kicking through a sprawling encampment of displaced, angry android veterans of the Robot Wars; and then a couple more hours trudging through uneven hills of sandy desert – all of which were done during a near whiteout – Chester A. Arthur XVII and Queen Victoria XXX finally found the abandoned spaceport in the southernmost fringes of Las Máquinas. They had been tasked with retrieving the trivection cooling unit, and stealing a thirty-year-old suborbital space plane was the only way to get to England that didn't involve swimming across a mostly dried-up ocean.

More importantly though, Chester A. Arthur XVII and Queen Victoria XXX found an unattended maintenance shed with a working shower, a cot, a space heater, a refrigerator with a bunch of unmarked lunches, and a large window that faced a small camp of homeless astronauts.

Discretion and a lack of a signed disclosure agreement forbid discussion of what exactly went on in that maintenance shed, save that it involved the shower, the stares of the homeless astronauts, the shower wall, the cot, a few lengths of bungee cord, a bench, some extraordinary flexibility and ingenuity on the part of Queen Victoria XXX, a jar of maple syrup, a very thorough inspection and appreciation of the newly non-robotic body of Chester A. Arthur XVII, the windowsill, some more gymnastics on the part of Queen Victoria XXX, some curling toes, some heaving breaths, a nap, and then the shower again, this time with a drop cloth thrown over the window.

Twenty minutes after that, the cloned queen and the remade president were in the lower part of the thermosphere of Earth, having stolen and hotwired a derelict low-orbit spacecraft, acts which required significantly less thought and effort than anything they had done in the shed.

CHAPTER THIRTY-EIGHT:
LAST TRAIN TO CLARKSVILLE

ALI ŞAHIN, CATRINA DALISAY AND BOUDICA IX stood huddled around a burning trash can on a desolate, damaged train platform on the outskirts of a desolate, damaged city just off the desolate, damaged interstate in the middle of a desolate, damaged desert. They had been forced to abandon the warmth and armor and remarkably deep MP3 collection of Charlie's tank several miles east of the city when its engines seized up and died. A cursory investigation, and a hard-coded fear of it being anything else, led them to diagnose the problem as a simple lack of fuel. Boudica IX did her best to get them a few more miles, but her farts were far too sporadic and uncontrolled to be counted on for more than that. Ultimately, try as the trio might – and try they did – without Thor they simply didn't have the intestinal fortitude or undiagnosed digestive issues necessary to pass enough gas to power the methane engine of the vehicle.

The donut merchant, the hotel employee, and the re-created Celt shivered beneath the benighted sky, soaked from the thighs down after slogging through miles of wet, packed snow, waiting for a train they weren't even sure would come. Dr. Arahami's only two parkas lost in the supply run to Los Alamos, the women stood in little more than heavy sweaters, while the skinny dark-skinned man shook slightly beneath his fleece sweatshirt. The trio pressed against the flaming trash can, the pain of the burning metal scarring their legs almost indistinguishable from the hypothermia. Often they leaned directly over the fire, inadvertently singing off stray hairs or eyebrows.

With the power out, the arrivals board was useless, and the only brochures the three found were a jumble of out-of-date maps and complex algebra problems. They knew they were somewhere between the city-states of Phoenix and Las Vegas, though whether they were on the edge of Las Máquinas, in the heart of the unforgiving geriatric stronghold of the Arizona territory, lost somewhere in one of the sweeping Mormon reservations, or standing squarely on some piece of contested land in between, they didn't know. Only time, and whether they got murdered or converted to a new religion, would tell.

CHAPTER THIRTY-NINE:
HE'S THE FATHER OF ALL LIES, AND THE UNCLE OF ALL CONVOLUTED SCHEMES

THE GREY-HAIRED MAN IN THE CRAPPY SUIT crouched in the snow, a hand on the nearby wooden fence post for balance, speaking slowly and softly through the razor wire fence to the rash of albino wolverines growling before him.

"... and then you need to gnaw on the foundation of *that* building until it collapses, too."

The unmistakable *clack* of a shotgun being chambered echoed behind the man's head, despite there only being a mess of furry carnivores and a very sharp fence for the sound to echo off of.

"What in the sugar-frosted fuck are you doing with my wolverines?" said someone behind the man in the suit – presumably, he thought, the same someone holding a shotgun against his skull.

"I can explain, miss," said the leather-faced weasel whisperer, his voice trembling. He stood slowly and placed his clearly empty hands behind his head.

"Turn around."

The man did as instructed, his body as shaky as his voice, turning eye-to-gun-barrel-to-eye with the shotgun wielder, a busty brunette in a fur-lined greatcoat.

"Persephone?" he asked, tilting his head around the weapon to get a better look.

"Lucy?" replied the woman, doing the same. "Is that you?"

"Please don't call me that," said the man with a confidence uncommon in someone with a gun in his face. His sleazy salesman air had disappeared. Even his suit looked better.

"You walked out on me. I'll call you whatever I want."

"It's Satan, Seph," grumbled the man in the suit, lowering his hands slightly. "You know I prefer Satan."

"What are you doing with my wolverines?" she asked, the shotgun still pointed directly at Satan's face.

"I didn't know they were yours. I promise. I only came to borrow them for a little while. There are a few nearby buildings I need gone and these guys are small enough to get under the napalm fences and angry enough to get past the armed elephant guards."

"You can't have them," the former Greek goddess snarled.

"What do you need wolverines for, Seph? You can lay curses down on mankind with the snap of your fingers."

"You know I don't know how to snap!" Persephone shoved both barrels of the gun against the grizzled man's nose.

"I can get you your powers back," he offered, his voice calm and collected, although somewhat squeakier than usual.

"If you could do that you wouldn't have a gun up your nostrils."

"I promise I will reimburse you should anything happen."

"That's not going to help me while they're gone."

"I can get you a job, with me, instead."

"Snap, crackle, bullshit, Lucy. You're a professional liar, even without your powers. You think I'm going to believe anything you say? Knowing who you are? What you did to me?"

"If you wanted me dead I'd be dead, Seph. Put the gun down." Satan slowly and deliberately pulled a fancy-looking business card from the interior pocket of his suit. He handed it to Persephone. "Here. I wasn't lying about the job thing."

Persephone took the card with her free hand and read it thoroughly, several times. Eventually she lowered her shotgun from Satan's face and tucked the weapon under her arm.

"For real, Lucy? You can set me up."

"You know I'm not one for props," he explained, thumbing gun oil from his nose. "I'm one hundred percent on the level. About this anyway, right now. Give me a hand with a few errands and I can get you in as a vice president. No more wolverine farming for you."

"I don't farm them. The wolverines are here to keep the underground moose away from the steak-o'-lanterns."

"The what?"

"They're meat-filled pumpkins."

"That sounds awful."

"They are. But people buy them." Persephone shook her head. "Fucking mortals."

The goddess of the underworld squinted at the card one more time, her dark eyes glinting, then flicked the edge with her finger.

"You can really get me in with him. For life?"

"Forever," replied Satan, smiling. "Once I put these last few parts in motion, we're golden."

"Last few..." began Persephone, gears clicking. "Are you the reason I've been living by candlelight for the last month?"

"No, the blackout was simply the impetus for the idea, a stroke of good luck. I had nothing to do with it, swear to whoever," the former ruler of Hell explained. "I may have had a hand in plunging the world headfirst into a new ice age, though."

"Pele[21]?"

"She is so easy to get riled up."

"So then the wolverines are for... Atomodynamics, down the road a spell? And Magma Machines Incorporated?"

"Among others."

"That's a lot of strings you're pulling, Lucy."

"That's kind of what I do."

The brunette glared at the grey-haired man standing before her.

"Can you guarantee I'm not going to regret this?"

"I can guarantee you anything you want."

Persephone raised the shotgun again.

"I'm sorry," said Satan, lifting his hands, "force of habit. In all seriousness, Seph: There is no way this plan can fail."

CHAPTER FORTY:
LONG WAY TO THE TOP

AMEN-RA, FORMER EGYPTIAN CREATOR of the universe and God-King of the Sun, was leaning back in his executive chair, his feet on his enormous mahogany desk. A half-empty jug of fortified beer sat pooling in itself next to the phone. The expansive office was comfortably warm, honest-to-goodness sunlight flooding in through the large glass walls, and Ra, finished with his appointments for the day, had taken off his jacket and tie and settled in for a rejuvenating nap. His pet lioness, Bambi, was doing the same, curled on the carpet at the front of his desk.

Ra was the owner and CEO of Heliopolis, the world's largest solar panel manufacturer. The sun god had started the business several years earlier – shortly after mathematics had put the beatdown on organized religion and he was cast down from Aaru, the Field of Reeds – back when he was nothing more than a confused, alcoholic has-been. And now look at him, he was fond of saying, a successful, alcoholic entrepreneur! Hell, the greatest alcoholic entrepreneur of all time!

The trick, as Ra always said, had been the willingness to work hard, the integrity to never give up, and, after he had nearly driven the first iteration of the company into the ground through mismanagement and shoddy investing, the ability to get stupid, sloppy drunk and accidentally tap into your latent deific powers and inundate your immediate delivery area with constant, abundant sunshine. Easy-peasy.

The most recent solar storm, the one that caused the blackout that was still wreaking havoc over the rest of the planet, had been a boon to Heliopolis. While other manufacturers' solar panels had shattered or melted, Heliopolis' Ra's Finest™ brand solar panels had thrived. When the ejection of solar energy hit them, they actually began to run *more* efficiently than before. And they were already the world leader in efficiency.

As people scrounged for every bit of energy they could find, trying to thwart the ongoing power outage, word spread about Heliopolis' nigh-immortal panels, sales skyrocketed, and Ra remembered how to party like a god-king should. Even when the volcanic winter showed up to drop a deuce in his orgy, blocking the sun and rendering Heliopolis' solar panels inoperable, Ra wouldn't let it stop him. Raising his middle fingers to the sky, he burned away the clouds of ash for a thousand miles in every direction from the headquarters of Heliopolis. The sun had shined nonstop ever since, its warm brilliance radiating down on Egypt like a heat lamp over a fast food cheeseburger.

Someone timidly knocked on the office door.

"Come in," boomed Ra, opening a single eye.

The door opened slowly and a tiny, frail old man in a jumpsuit shuffled a few steps into the room.

"S-S-Sir," he said, shaking like a chihuahua in a snowstorm, "there's-there's been an inc-c-cident."

CHAPTER FORTY-ONE:
THE LITTLE ENGINE THAT COULD

AFTER WHAT FELT LIKE SEVERAL HOURS – mostly because it had been several hours – the faint sound of a train whistle drifted across the empty platform and Ali, Catrina, and Boudica IX emerged from their shuddering, half-dead stupor. Turning and squinting into the distance they could just make out the lights of the oncoming train. The locomotive approached quickly, its constant plume of white steam nearly lost in the sheets of frozen moisture falling from the grey sky.

Somewhere deep in the linty back pockets of their minds, the trio knew that this train was all that separated them from retrieving the spork-headed screwdriver and the isotonium, that the fate of the continent's ability to run a hair dryer or play Angry Birds again rested on this single locomotive. Mostly though, they were hoping the train had a toilet and a temperature warm enough to let them thaw their bodily fluids and use it.

The steam engine eased into the station, car after car crawling past Ali, Catrina, and Boudica IX. As the train came to a complete stop, a heavily-fortified door slid open directly in front of the threesome.

The cyborg, the girl, and the clone were shuttled onboard by the most efficient and courteous conductor ever known to mankind. With a disconcertingly genuine smile, the man waived their fares due to their dire state, assured them the train – despite its circuitous and slipshod route – made stops in both the ruins of San Francisco and the territory of Irish Colombia, and then made sure to point out the lack of emergency exits, as the train was not only zombie-repellant, but also atomic mutant-proof and werewolf-resistant. He led them to an empty car, waved them into their seats, handed out blankets, and then, with a bow and an even greater smile than before, resumed his rounds and disappeared into the next car.

The interior of the railroad car was gloriously overdone, with ornate wood paneling and solid gold trim, heavy burgundy curtains hanging from the windows, and bright red crushed velvet seats with enough leg room for a professional basketball team. There was not a single empty beer can or Styrofoam cup to be found rolling around the floor or wedged between a plush armrest and the wall, and no part of the locomotive smelled like urine – not even the bathroom.

With only the slightest of lurches, the train departed from the ramshackle station. Boudica IX sprawled across three seats, while, across the aisle, Catrina was nestled into Ali's side, several blankets wrapped tightly around her.

CHAPTER FORTY-TWO:
EAT IT, EVERYONE WHO ISN'T AN ANCIENT EGYPTIAN SUN GOD

RA THREW OPEN THE DOORS to the factory floor, the metal swinging back and clanging off the concrete walls. Blazing white sunlight streamed across the manufacturing plant from behind his tensed body, glistening off conveyer belts and panel stacks and all the blood.

"What," roared the sun god, his voice violently echoing off every corner and shaking the overhead lights, "is going on in here?"

Everything before him stopped, even the machinery. The factory floor was a statuary of incredibly loyal workers and shambling, homicidal mummies mid-grapple, fists resting in faces and teeth pausing atop forearms. Here and there amidst the carnage were dwarves in cowboy hats riding large jackals, clearly responsible for herding the mummies into the factory.

Ra raised a hand and the light behind him became blinding, a whiteout that seemed to erase the building. As the sunshine faded back into something more agreeable to the human visible spectrum, the mummies collapsed to the floor in dusty heaps, their smoldering, emaciated bodies crumbling apart like dried-out sand sculptures. The workers, for their part, were only temporarily blind and severely sunburned.

"I repeat," snarled Ra, eyeing the nearest dwarf, "what is going on in here?"

"He— He said we had to get rid of all the competing energy companies," whimpered the little man.

"He? He who?" Ra made this sound significantly more threatening than one would think would be possible, given the syntax.

"Shut *up*, Murray," stage whispered another dwarf.

"Tell me who!"

"He'll kill us!" a third dwarf quietly shouted.

"He— He has a plan," stammered Murray. "He said he wants to be— to be the only energy provider available, anywhere, of any kind!"

"Give me a name!" demanded the CEO. Small cracks zigzagged across the factory walls.

"His name– His name is –"

"Don't do it, Murray!"

The hyenas looked at one another, winked in series, and then proceeded to maul the dwarven cowboys before Murray, or any of them, could rat out the man who had paid the man who had paid the hyenas handsomely in rotting animal carcasses.

"Trying to create a monopoly, are you?" thundered Ra, god of the sun, to no one in particular. His eyes narrowed. "Good luck with that, asshole."

With nary but a tremendous sense of outrage and spite, Ra raised his arms and the sun glowed white hot again. The factory workers winced and covered their eyes once more, ducking behind machinery to hide from the ever-present radiance. Cups of cold coffee began to boil, Post-It notes burst into flames.

Blinding sunshine burst across the entirety of the planet like a door being opened onto the sidewalk outside of a movie theater. Within minutes, the global volcanic winter disappeared.

CHAPTER FORTY-THREE:
IS TEMPERATURE WHIPLASH A THING?

"THIS MAY TAKE LONGER THAN DRIVING, but at least it's warm in here," Catrina said, her face buried in the armpit of Ali's hooded sweatshirt. "I think my blood was starting to freeze."

"I don't think we're gonna have to worry about that anymore," said Boudica IX, prone across an entire row, her feet dangling in the aisle and her eyes looking awkwardly through the window just above her.

The counterfeit Celtic queen pointed toward the rapidly dissipating clouds and the effulgently white sun burning them away. Daylight screamed in through every window and turned the train car into a sauna in seconds.

"Am I seriously too warm now?" Ali mumbled incredulously, lifting his sweatshirt and fanning the fabric against his stomach. "Is that what's happening, or did the frostbite get into my brain?"

"Son of a bitch," muttered Catrina, kicking off her blankets and wriggling out of her sweater.

A set of speakers, lodged above the etched-glass bifold doors on either end of the railcar, crackled.

"Well, folks," said an overly cheery voice through the train's PA, "as you all may have noticed, it appears the weather has suddenly decided to take a turn for the beautiful and bathe us all in some much-needed sunshine. It appears our long frozen nightmare is finally over. That said, we would like to take this opportunity to apologize in advance, as the next several legs of our trip are unfortunately going to have to be without air conditioning. We did not anticipate the volcanic winter lifting, remarkable though it is and grateful though we are, and left our station of origin without the necessary coolants or motors to get the AC purring for you the way you'd surely like. With your best interests in mind, of course, we thought removing all that heavy equipment might make the train a little lighter and save you all a few minutes of travel time and get you to our destinations faster. You'll have to trust us that it seemed like a good idea at the time.

"Looks like Mother Nature showed us, though, right? Anyway, folks, again, we extend our deepest sympathies and, to make up for the oversight, coffee's on us for the rest of your trip."

CHAPTER FORTY-FOUR:
HERE COMES THE SUN

SATAN'S HUMMER IDLED ON THE SIDE of the abandoned interstate. Persephone and the Prince of Lies sat in the front seats, staring disbelievingly through the windshield at the wall of sunshine barreling towards them, shaving away the volcanic winter like so much cumulonimbic stubble.

"I thought you said –"

"Shut up."

CHAPTER FORTY-FIVE:
THIS JUST IN

"THIS IS DOUGLAS RANCH WAGON for KOAT, Albuquerque's most-trusted news source, with your evening update.

"Now that the neverending dark has mysteriously vanished – and with it, the high-piled snow and the roving herds of angry, angry polar bears – society, it appears, is no longer afraid to go outside. Perhaps more surprisingly, though, is the fact that while stumbling around out there, trying to remember that the sun is not some terrible burning lesion afflicting the sky, we seem to have remembered that even though the electrical grid is down and our telecommunications satellites are still orbiting husks of scrap metal, we, as a people, can still see. Our eyes are still fine – unless you're blind, of course. As such, society has rediscovered how to use the semaphore system to communicate with one other, sometimes as far as all the way down the block.

"Communications are spotty, thus far, as this reporter, along with many others, had no idea that semaphore was an actual thing and learned what to do from a book that he had previously been using as both a source of fiber and toilet paper. Likewise, this reporter, and others, did not have the correct flags, so he has been using soiled clothing and torn-up paintings from the lobby.

"Still, with lines of sight restored and everyone desperate to know if he or she is the last man or woman standing, thereby solidifying his or her claim as the pinnacle of creation and the undisputed winner of the human race, communications have been swift, albeit clunky and probably occasionally inaccurate.

"Barring any kind of misinterpretation or blatantly misleading reporting by those jerks at the radio station, the top story appears to be the astonishing number of attacks on energy concerns by teams of cryptids, ghosts, and some of our more unscrupulous genetically-altered animals. The attacks have all been unprovoked, though presumably they are all related. My professional opinion is that this is the Milton Bradley war machine spooling up, desperate to keep us all in the boring, internet-less dark and force us to play their crappy board games over and over again.

"In local news, I am still trapped in the KOAT building, as an overturned bus is blocking the only exit.

"Turning now to household hints. Narrating your every thought into a battery-operated recorder is a great way to give your loved ones the gift of documentation of your final hours, leaving them evidence and closure when they inevitably eventually find your naked body drowned in a ladies room toilet. This advice comes to you from Bruce, who seemed pretty with it up until he killed himself this morning after not seeing the sun for over a week. If only you'd held out a little longer, buddy.

"Be sure to check back for the nightly news a little later, once I search through that semaphore book and figure out what left, right, left, right, up, down, flag thrown off the side of the building means. I'll also have some new recipes for sun-roasted Bruce.

"This has been Douglas Ranch Wagon for KOAT, Albuquerque's handsomest news source."

CHAPTER FORTY-SIX:
CONCERT HALLS SHMONCERT SHMALLS, HE'S STILL AN ASSHOLE

THE GHOST OF ANDREW CARNEGIE had been tasked with taking out the DiNoCo power station a few miles east of the Erie Canal. A simple enough chore. Carnegie was more than adept at ridding the world of smaller competitors and leveling the playing field for those few large corporations that truly deserved it. Not to mention, now that he was already dead, he didn't have to hide his ruthlessness behind all that philanthropic bullshit. Perhaps most importantly of all, though, Andrew Carnegie had already flooded two other hydroelectric plants along the lake that very morning. Taking out DiNoCo should have been quick and simple.

"Should" being the word Andrew Carnegie was most annoyed with.

DiNoCo was not, in fact, another hydroelectric plant, and the capital "N" in the middle of the signage atop the building was more for style than anything. If Carnegie had been able to see the incorporation papers, he would have known that DiNoCo was actually called DinoCo, which might have tipped him off to the fact that there were seven starved, frothing giganotosaurus[22] inside.

The giganotosaurus were all wearing large wool sweaters and thick cotton booties, and every surface of the room was carpeted in deep shag. The thundering reptiles were chained to a number of electrical conductors hidden in the corners, those conductors attached to large turbines outside. The dinosaurs' massive girth and frantic, plodding movements were creating heretofore unseen levels of static electricity and powering two nearby villages.

Andrew Carnegie had been expecting an empty dam, or, at best, a mostly empty dam with an old security guard, and, for that reason, had brought only a knife. Finding seven of the most perfect killing machines that ever lived in front of him, he suddenly felt woefully inadequate. Still, Andrew Carnegie was a man of his word, especially when that word involved destroying small businesses for the sake of letting a giant corporation get a monopoly on energy.

The ghost of Andrew Carnegie – possessing the first dead hobo he had seen – attacked the dinosaurs four times, stabbing repeatedly into their cotton-swathed ankles, before any of them even noticed. Once they did, they made short work of devouring the hobo's body.

Andrew Carnegie was left standing ethereal and knifeless, and not entirely sure what to do next.

Thankfully Mark Hughes and Timmy the super-squirrel appeared to help the deceased industrialist figure that out.

"What the fuck is going on here?" demanded an enraged Timmy.

"I... uh... you see..." the ghost stammered.

"These animals are being exploited!" The squirrel gestured toward the dinosaurs. "This isn't right!"

"Oh, that? That wasn't me. I was actually sent here to set them free. Incidentally, really, as a side effect of destroying this place. But, still, I'm on the dinosaurs' side. Promise."

"Are you the asshole who's been running up and down the lake flooding everything?" asked Mark.

"Maybe," replied Andrew Carnegie noncommittally. "That really depends on what you're doing here. I'm less certain how I'm supposed to be playing this now."

"You're crippling these communities," Mark seethed. "The people who didn't drown outright are going to starve. Or die of heat stroke. There are a lot of old people up here! It's a miracle they survived this long. Taking away their air conditioning now is just mean."

"Really? Morals? That's how you're pitching your side?" countered the ghost. "I sold out the city of Pittsburgh and turned it into a Tolkein-esque nightmare of industrialization and lung cancer. You think I have problems taking money from a corporate donor and smashing the shit out of small businesses? I *invented* that."

Timmy grabbed the ghost with his mind. Slowly, the squirrel began stretching the industrialist, his ethereal frame twisting and thinning and beginning to unravel.

"Bloody hell!"

"You can unravel ghosts?" Mark asked out of the corner of his mouth.

"Apparently," said Timmy with a tiny shrug. "I honestly didn't know if this was going to work." He rolled the ghost into a circle, Andrew Carnegie's feet merging with his head.

"Knock it off!" shouted the dead industrialist.

"Who sent you?" the squirrel demanded. "What the hell is going on? Why are all these tiny, bullshit alternative energy companies being attacked?"

"I don't –"

The super-powered rodent wrung the spirit like a wet sponge.

"Some guy!" shouted the spiraled ghost of Andrew Carnegie, his voice warbling uncontrollably. "Old guy in a suit, grey hair, wrinkled as the day is long. He asked if I wanted to wreck up some mom-and-pop energy shops and I said yes."

"Why?" barked the squirrel, balling the ghost up like a used tissue.

"I don't know! I didn't care!"

"What's his plan? Where's he going next?" asked Mark.

"I honestly don't know. He told me to stay up here, near the Pretty Good Lakes, so I didn't get in anyone else's way. He's hiring tons of us. I don't –"

Timmy shoved Andrew Carnegie's head up his own ass.

"WANG!" the ghost shouted from deep within his own ethereal bowels. "He said something about WANG Electric!"

The squirrel removed the man's head from his anus.

"He said... he said he was going there later. That's honestly all I know."

"Worldwide Atlanta Natural Gas and Electric?" said Mark. "The huge corporation that supplies gas and electricity to the Southeast[23]?"

"With the main electrical grid out, the company he works for saw a chance to make a power grab. I don't think the pun was intentional."

"That's impossible," continued the cyborg.

"No one could make a pun that bad by accident!" shouted the squirrel, folding the ghost into an origami crane.

"No, I meant the power grab part," replied Mark. "There's hundreds, if not thousands, of energy concerns and corporations. Not to mention that the grid is being repaired as we speak."

"Oh, right."

"It's being repaired?" the ghost parroted.

"You didn't know that?"

"No."

"Does the old guy?" asked Mark.

"He didn't mention it," answered the ghost, shrugging his wings. Noticing the concerned looks on the faces of his captors, he added, "I promise I won't tell. Please don't kill me."

"Kill you?"

"You're already dead," said Timmy.

At that point the telekinetic squirrel disassembled the ghost of Andrew Carnegie, turning his ethereal spirit into so much incorporeal confetti.

"I guess we're going to Atlanta," said Mark. "See if we can catch this guy and figure out what's going on."

"God damn it," replied Timmy.

"It's the Paris of the South."

"That is a lie and you fucking know it."

"We have to find out what this is all about, Timmy, and this is the best lead we've gotten so far. All those mermaids went on about was injustice and environmentalism. And I don't even know what that roc[24] was saying."

"His accent was impenetrable."

"Look, if it's any consolation, I hear Atlanta's a lot nicer, now that the House of Waffle has been deposed."

"Have they gotten the dried eggs off everything?"

"Not everything, no."

"What about the smell?"

"Burnt coffee. Unless it's windy. Then you get the whiskey shits."

"And the thick, greasy air?"

"We have to go, Timmy."

The squirrel sighed. "Fine. Let me just set these guys free first."

"What did I just tell him?! You can't —"

With a thought, Timmy the super-squirrel snapped the enormous metal chains holding the giganotosaurus to the walls. The shackles fell to the ground, sparking with static electricity. The dinosaurs were free. The giant carnivorous reptiles showed their appreciation by roaring thunderously and immediately lumbering towards the squirrel and the cyborg.

"Oh, right," thought Timmy. "They're dinosaurs."

"We should probably run."

CHAPTER FORTY-SEVEN:
TILTING AT WINDMILLS

"TYPHOID" MARY MALLON AND Lizbeth "Lizzie" Borden — both possessing the mummified and appropriately adorned corpses of Spanish conquistadors, stolen from a nearby traveling history circus — knocked over the last of the windmills with tedious sighs.

"Again I ask, are you sure we must honor our agreement with that grey-haired gentleman?" Lizbeth queried, staring forlornly at the toppled masses of wooden blades and supports strewn across the hillside before her. "Our sexual escapades notwithstanding, this is all becoming rather boring."

"I am less and less certain, my dear," replied Mary, placing her lanky arms on her armored hips. "We agreed to his request out of sadistic fervor, not some pedestrian adoration of wanton destruction. I thought that with the return of the fair weather we might finally see again some opposition and satiate our bloodlust."

"Maybe it would be for the best if we retired from this request and waylaid the mutant camp we passed earlier."

"Oh, but they looked so distraught. The battle would hardly be fair."

"There would at least be blood."

"Green blood," scoffed Mary. "The stuff is foul-smelling at best."

"Well then, Mary, I am not sure what to —"

A large boulder fell from the sky, crushing the diminutive frame of Lizbeth's host corpse into an armored pile and catching the ghost by surprise. She turned her ethereal head upward.

"What in the world?"

"Pteranodons," grumbled Mary, lowering the crusty eyelids of her gangly conquistador. Another boulder slammed into the ground near her feet.

"Did we awaken a nest? There are so many that they are blotting out the sky!"

"The only nest around here is gonna be the one they make outta your bones," a commanding voice boomed.

The ghost and the deceased Spaniard lowered their heads and found an armed mob marching on them. They were armed stereotypically, with pitchforks and torches and sages who could commune with pteranodons. A lot of them were also in slippers or behind aluminum walkers with tennis balls on the feet.

"Sister," snarled the leathery old man in the fedora at the front of the mob, "you picked the wrong wind-powered retirement community to fuck with."

The man pulled a revolver from the elastic waistband of his sweat-pants and fired a bullet squarely between Mary's eyes, collapsing the decomposing skull of the conquistador and leaving Mary's ethereal old lady face floating above the shoulders of a headless corpse.

"I do think they mean to fight us," said Mary, smiling.

"Well it is about damned time," replied Lizbeth.

CHAPTER FORTY-EIGHT: A WELL-HUNG JUDGE, JURY, AND EXECUTIONER

CHESTER A. ARTHUR XVII AND Queen Victoria XXX sat strapped into the stolen spaceplane, the LEDs and assorted –ometers of the control panel blinking and sparking before them. Thick dust billowed around the aircraft, obscuring their view, as tiny chunks of sheetrock and clay tile continuously fell, lightly *plinking* off the cockpit glass. Hidden behind the dust cloud were bits and pieces, large and small, of the roof and one of the bedrooms of the Earl of New London.

"What the fuck was that, Charlie?"

"You said you didn't want to walk."

With a skin-tingling metallic screech, the spaceplane lurched forward awkwardly, digging itself deeper into the mansion of Tyrone Tainthammer. A large piece of unseen furniture toppled loudly to the floor.

"I said I didn't want to walk *far*," replied Queen Victoria XXX. "I didn't say I wanted you to crash into a building."

"I didn't crash," said Chester A. Arthur XVII indignantly. "We made a three point landing. It's not my fault his roof was so shoddily constructed that it couldn't handle the weight of a single two-person sub-orbital aircraft."

"Are you calling me fat?"

"What?! No, I –"

"I'm messing with you, Charlie." The queen smiled. "I wanted to see if maybe Joselin gave you a sense of humor this time around."

"Ha ha," he stated.

"No, *hahahahaha*," she countered, laughing uncontrollably.

"What's gotten into you?"

"Well, you, to be perfectly blunt," said Queen Victoria XXX. She looked at her boyfriend, searching for some glimmer of amusement at the statement. Not finding it, she continued. "Plus I'm pretty sure there hasn't been a lot of oxygen for the last couple hours."

"I think there might have been a problem with the artificial atmosphere controls."

It was at that moment that a cane with an obscenely large diamond handle was rapped against the outside of the cockpit. Looking toward the sound, the two clones were just able to see a scrawny, middle-aged white guy in a thick, tremendously gaudy bathrobe – with an unnecessarily high fur collar – standing in the swirling dust beside the spaceplane. Chester A. Arthur XVII pressed a button and the glass of the cockpit jerkily slid backward.

"You two care t' explain why there's a 'ole in my ceiling and a plane in one of my spare bedrooms?" asked the man in the bathrobe.

"Are you Tyrone Tainthammer?" inquired the reconstituted president.

"In the prodigious flesh."

"Really?" asked Queen Victoria XXX, leaning around Chester A. Arthur XVII and squinting her eyes. "Not to get all racist or anything, but I was expecting a large, chiseled black man. You are incredibly disappointing."

"I'm black where it counts, love."

"I don't know if you can say that."

"No, I've checked, I'm all right."

The dust cleared slightly, enough to reveal the half dozen large, chiseled men of all kinds of races standing behind the Earl of New London. The large, chiseled men also carried large, chiseled cudgels encrusted with large, chiseled jewels.

"Now, gettin' back t' the matter at hand," continued Tyrone Tainthammer, "why did you crash a plane into my mansion?"

"We didn't *crash* it," snarled Chester A. Arthur XVII.

***

"... and we need your trivection cooling unit to restore the North American electrical grid," explained Chester A. Arthur XVII, enjoying a, quite frankly, phenomenal cup of tea, despite the sharpened rubies being pressed against the back of his neck by way of an oversized club.

The genetically reconstructed president, Queen Victoria XXX, and Tyrone Tainthammer, retired porn star and Earl of New London, were sitting on a pair of floral print settees that cost more than the gross national product of several small countries, in a similarly decored drawing room that could have housed the refugees from several small countries that went bankrupt buying overly ornate furniture. Surrounding the trio on all sides – as well as from the adjoining doorways, the staircase, and the hallways that overlooked the room – were several dozen of the broadest, thickest, most Brobdingnagian men in existence, standing with their arms crossed. With the exception of the one holding a jewel-encrusted club to Chester A. Arthur XVII, the men didn't appear to be armed, but that didn't appear to matter much.

"Well, ain't that interestin'," said Tyrone Tainthammer. "Problem is, it's *my* cooling unit. I went through a lot of trouble t' get it and I'm rather fond of the thing. I'm not about to 'and it over simply 'cause you say please."

"Pretty please?" added Queen Victoria XXX.

"The welfare of the entire North American continent depends on us bringing the trivection cooling unit back," said Chester A. Arthur XVII. "Thousands upon thousands of lives are hanging on this."

"Oh, well, when you put it that way," said the Earl of New London, "no."

"You're going to let all those people die? All so you don't have to part with a single piece of your industrial machinery collection?"

"That's about the long an' short of it, yeah," continued the scrawny man in the bathrobe. "Your people aren't my problem. I don't really give a lick what 'appens to 'em. I've got an entire island full of my own people, trustin' in me and, more importantly, fearin' me. I can't be lookin' soft in front of 'em."

"You can't be serious! A third of the world's population is at risk and you're worried about appearances?"

"Oh, come off it. *The power's out.* They'll figger out 'ow to build windmills sooner or later. Humans 've been doin' it for 'undreds of years."

"I don't think you understand how lazy most North Americans are."

Queen Victoria XXX groaned. "Cut the bullshit, Charlie. We're just as lazy as all those other jerks back home. Tyrone's completely right. We could rejigger the grid to run on literally anything else, but we don't want to because that might take more than an afternoon. The only reason we're here is because of your hero complex and because the thought of actual manual labor bores the ever-loving shit out of me."

"But all those people —" began Chester A. Arthur XVII.

"Are either dead already or they're not," said the cloned queen. "Honestly, if they can't handle the lights being out without offing themselves, I'm not sure we really want them around."

"OK, sure, but the winter put a lot of extra stress on at-risk persons and without electricity there's no heat which —"

"Doesn't mean ass right now. The winter's over. It's been eighty degrees and sunny from Las Máquinas to New London and everywhere else we could see from that spaceplane, which was at least half the planet."

"Well, yeah, but..."

The reconstituted royal sighed. "Will you please just admit you're an opportunistic narcissist so we can get on with this?"

"'Opportunistic narcissist' is a little harsh," said Chester A. Arthur XVII.

"If the shoe fits, love," added Tyrone Tainthammer.

"OK, fine," said the president begrudgingly. "Can we please have the trivection cooling unit because we want the trivection cooling unit? There are no moral implications at play, it would simply make our lives a lot easier."

"Thank you. I appreciate your 'onesty. But the answer's still no."

"Oh come on!" barked Queen Victoria XXX. "Didn't you hear how lazy we were?"

"We have money," said Chester A. Arthur XVII. "Can we just buy the damn thing from you?"

"Why would I possibly need money?" asked Tyrone Tainthammer, spreading his arms and gesturing toward the extravagant mansion and the dozens of hired goons surrounding them. "You think these blokes are 'ere out of the goodness of their 'earts?"

"I am," said one of the goons, raising a hand the size of a ham steak.

"Look," continued the earl, "easiest thing t' do would be for you two t' give up, walk out the front door, and switch over that grid t' a wind farm like the lady was goin' on about. Judgin' from that fire in your eyes, though, retreat i'n't in your wheelhouse. So you could try punchin' your way into gettin' what you want..." He again indicated the mountainous men surrounding them. "... though I don't recommen' that."

"They don't look that big," said Queen Victoria XXX, stealthily slipping her hand under her dress and onto the grip of her revolver.

"I wouldn' do that, love." The Earl of New London threw back the edge of his bathrobe, revealing the handgun strapped to his own thigh, as well as some other intimidating artillery.

"Holy shit. You weren't kidding."

"I like you," said the scrawny man, closing his bathrobe back up and spreading his arms along the top of the settee. "The both of you. So 'ere's what I'm proposin'. Be in my new film."

"We're not doing a porno," said Chester A. Arthur XVII.

"At least not one that anyone else is gonna be aware of," added the queen quietly.

"It's not porn, I've moved on from that," explained Tyrone Tainthammer with a dismissive wave of his hand. "Lost my passion for the genre. Plus adult films just aren't lucrative anymore. What people want now is 'eart and soul. Danger. They want to be moved, not just aroused. 'S why my newest venture is point-of-view action-adventure-romantic-comedy. Two lovers meetin' and fallin' in love and riskin' everythin' to be together at all costs. All wit' cameras strapped to their heads. That way the audience can feel every moment of the thing. They can live the movie."

Queen Victoria XXX shrugged. "That could be fun. I'm in."

"What if we gave you the sub-orbital aircraft?" asked Chester A. Arthur XVII.

"You already did."

"What're you, camera shy?" the artificial royal teased.

"You know I can't act," mumbled the patchwork president.

"Oh, crap, right," said Queen Victoria XXX, suddenly remembering. She turned towards the earl. "He's not lying. We tried to role-play a couple times but he's so awful I actually lost wood. I couldn't have boned him if I wanted to, which I didn't because he was so terrible. I almost threw up."

"Won't be a problem, love," said Tyrone Tainthammer.

"You're sure?" asked Chester A. Arthur XVII. "Because I almost vomited myself."

"Trus' me. I 'ave a way of bringin' out the best in people. But there's always the leavin' or the punchin' if you'd rather."

The reconstituted American politician furrowed his brow. "This isn't much of an offer."

"More of a formality, really," said the Earl of New London. "To make myself feel better 'bout how it all played out."

CHAPTER FORTY-NINE:
THE GREAT TRAIN ROBBERY

THE STEAM TRAIN CONTINUED ITS serpentine journey toward Irish Colombia and its requisite isotonium deposits, chugging along the western coastline of North America at a decent clip. Sweaty and half-dressed in the overly warm railcar, Catrina and Ali were nonetheless nestled against one another, leaning against one side of the train and staring absentmindedly out the opposite window at the landscapes that passed. Arid deserts turning into golden farmland turning into the most beautiful shoreline known to man, beast, or cab driver. Catrina's eyes began to drift shut, the sparkling dance of sunlight off the rippling deep blue ocean boring her into unconsciousness.

Ali, slightly less opposed to nature being beautiful, held out a little longer, until he too felt his eyes begin to close. The last thing he saw as his eyelids shut were twenty figures on horseback racing alongside the train.

The twenty figures on horseback were also the first thing he saw when he groggily reopened his eyes a moment later.

"Hey, look," he mumbled moonily. "Guys on horses."

Ali smiled slightly, fondly remembering weekend afternoons spent with his grandfather watching old Westerns. His eyes began to close once again.

Then he remembered what guys on horseback generally did to trains.

His eyes stayed open after that.

"Shit."

Ali craned his neck to look out the windows behind him. A small white circle inside of a larger green circle was there to meet him. Sliding out of his seat and adjusting his view, he realized a man wearing a ballistics vest and a motocross mask was pointing a rocket propelled grenade at the side of the train.

"SHIT."

Grabbing Catrina, Ali dove into the aisle of the railcar and began squirming forward, away from the bandits, rousing the tiny Filipina woman from her slumber, a fact she was neither fond of nor comfortable with. She shoved his hand away.

"Ali, what the hell are you –"

The wall they had just been leaning against exploded, raining crushed velvet seat cushions and flaming curtain remnants across the car.

"Shit?" she asked.

"Shit."

"Fuck."

The masked man with the RPG leapt from his horse – a bulging, veiny, steroid-riddled mustang with black racing stripes dyed into its red coat – and through the hole, landing in the train with a crouch. Two others followed. On the other side, a large wooden mallet was being swung at the window, buckling it inwards and loosing the reinforced glass from its mounting. Beneath the window was a sleeping Boudica IX.

"Bo!" shouted Catrina. "Bo! Wake up!"

From the next car up, Catrina and Ali could hear a commotion – voices screaming and glass shattering. From the car behind they saw the conductor and two of his colleagues marching toward them in full body armor and loading shotguns. They seemed to be extremely happy about the recent turn of events.

"No need to worry, folks," said the conductor, smiling. "We've got this all under control."

A half dozen shots rang out from the front car, six bullets simultaneously lodging into the chest plate of the conductor. He raised his shotgun and fired, directly over the heads of the donut merchant and the hotel employee. Behind him, his colleagues were grappling fiercely with the first three marauders, a flurry of elbows, fists, and at least one lead pipe. The window above Boudica IX popped inward, sailing over her prostrate body, followed by the hammer. A large man tried to clamber through the opening.

"What the hell, guys?" asked Catrina. "I thought you said this train was safe."

"From zombies, werewolves, and mutants," explained the conductor, reloading his shotgun. "We never said it was assholes-on-horses-proof."

There was a small explosion above them, a good chunk of the roof peeling away and bouncing along the tops of the remaining railcars. Three women in tactical jumpsuits dropped into the car, bandanas around their faces. The largest dropped directly behind the conductor and introduced herself by jamming a large knife through his neck.

As the man's body fell to the ground, Ali scrambled around it and grabbed the murderess' leg with his robotic arm. She looked down, her eyebrow cocked. The implant was vibrating imperceptibly, matching the woman's resonant frequency.

"What the fuck are you doing, kid?" she asked. Then her leg exploded into its component molecules, a fine pink mist splashing along the train's interior. The bandit screamed and collapsed to the ground.

Ali wiped the bloody particulate spray from his face with his human arm.

"This is why I hate public transportation," he said.

Catrina, meanwhile, had crawled forward, past the five marauders brawling with the two remaining conductors, and retrieved the original attacker's dropped RPG. Shouldering it, she leaned against the edge of the nearest intact row of seats and fired a grenade directly into the large bearded man who had finally almost made it through the window. The impact knocked him outside, where he and the grenade detonated. Boudica IX continued snoring.

"Wake the fuck up!" shouted Catrina.

CHAPTER FIFTY:
GRIZZLY MEN

TYRONE TAINTHAMMER LED Chester A. Arthur XVII and Queen Victoria XXX through his expansive mansion – past a heavily-draped piano room, a room full of monkeys smoking pipes and banging on typewriters, two sex dungeons, and a kitchen the size of a modest ranch house, the ghost of Julia Child shouting "Hulloo!" from behind a slab of raw apatosaurus meat – and into the attached film studio. In the center of the cavernous room was a single well-lit green screen, thinning rows of potted trees and shrubs flanking it on either side. On the runner of the screen, in the clearing between the shrubbery, sat a single blue Oldsmobile. Framed correctly, and with a twinkling cityscape projected onto the screen, the scene would have been highly evocative of a make-out point from any teen movie of the 1950s.

Except, of course, for the single, mournful, black, thirty-something man sprawled across the hood of the car and reading a vintage pornographic magazine. That man was Martin Van Buren XCIX, cloned brethren of Chester A. Arthur XVII and Queen Victoria XXX. Judging from his all black attire and the sullen demeanor apparent on his face, he was recently the perpetrator of a heist that went very badly.

"Marty?" called Chester A. Arthur XVII, squinting as he walked across the empty studio. "What the hell are you doing here?"

"Charlie?" replied Martin Van Buren XCIX, his eyebrow arched. "Same as you, I'm guessing. You guys trying to steal the tri-vection unit?"

"We were *trying*, yeah."

"Did you see the size of those guys out there? I punched one and fractured a couple knuckles. For an eighty-year-old porn star, this guy's remarkably on top of things."

"You're eighty?" gasped Queen Victoria XXX.

"What can I say, love?" Tyrone Tainthammer shrugged. "Hard livin' suits me."

"I would've said fifty, tops."

"Fifty? I must be losin' a step."

"For what it's worth," replied the queen, "I'm not good with ages. I mean, I'm technically only six years old."

"We all are," added Chester A. Arthur XVII.

"Bollocks," said Tyrone dismissively.

"No, seriously," called Martin Van Buren XCIX from the car. "A German sausage manufacturer created hundreds of us in vats after those gorillas blew up Washington, D.C."

"You do realize how ridiculous that sounds, yeah?"

Martin Van Buren XCIX shrugged. "You're an octogenarian porn star who successfully staged a militarized coup and took over England without ever putting on pants. I'd say we're even."

The trio finally arrived at the green screen. Chester A. Arthur XVII and Martin Van Buren XCIX man-hugged, patting one another on the back. The Earl of London was biting his lip thoughtfully.

"Six years old, eh? That could cause some problems for me."

"The kind of problems that would involve us being released?" proffered Chester A. Arthur XVII.

"Nah, course not," replied Tyrone Tainthammer. "I'll just 'ave to change distributors is all." The scrawny man in the bathrobe whistled and several hulking piles of men emerged from behind the green screen, checking the lighting, bringing out a trunk of period clothing, and wheeling cameras into position.

"Right, you two'll need to be removin' your trousers now," said the retired porn star, pointing toward the two former presidents. "You should be able to find somethin' more appropriate for the picture in that trunk."

"Us two?" asked Martin Van Buren XCIX.

"Yes, you two," explained Tyrone Tainthammer. "You two are the lovers."

Queen Victoria XXX began bouncing up and down and squealing with delight.

"Oh," said Chester A. Arthur XVII. "When you were telling us about it, I had assumed you meant me and Vicky."

"Tha's why you don' assume. Makes an ass out of you and me. Although, in this case, mostly you." The man in the bathrobe pointed his chin toward the presidents. "'urry up and get changed. This isn't the only picture I 'ave to film against people's wills today."

The artificial politicians began undressing, the Earl of London watching them in detached observation, with special emphasis on their bathing suit areas. A calculating look descended on his face, like an ambitious four-year-old staring at a pile of Lincoln Logs. Queen Victoria XXX was doing the same, though the look on her face more approximated a four-year-old being given a bag of sugar and a spoon.

This all stopped, of course, when a bellowing roar ripped across the film studio, shaking the rafters and knocking over some of the plants.

The clones turned, the men doing so awkwardly and with some difficulty, as their pants had only made it as far as their ankles. At the far end of the studio an enormous frothing werebear was being led across the expanse, pulled forward by chains. The men doing the pulling, as imposing as they were in their own right, looked positively adorable and unthreatening in view of the raging colossus behind them.

"What the fuck is that?" asked Martin Van Buren XCIX.

"That's the 'at all costs,'" said Tyrone Tainthammer. "I told you about that earlier, di'n't I?"

CHAPTER FIFTY-ONE: EMERGENCY EXIT

BOUDICA IX WAS FORCEFULLY GETTING a piggyback ride from one of the seemingly perpetual bandits assailing the train. Her legs clenched around his torso, the queen had one of her hands on both of his, firing the man's own gun into his compatriots, while the other hand slammed the man's head into any solid object she could find. On the far side of the car, the still shirtless Ali was busy dissolving marauders with his cybernetic arm in between bouts of very awkward and not always successful sword fighting.

The remade Celtic warrior-queen shoved the masked man's head into the twisted metal edge of the exploded wall before dismounting with a flourish and kicking him into the charging legs of the steroid-powered horses still running parallel to the train. Leaning out the hole and looking toward the front of the locomotive, Boudica IX watched as another pack of bandits on horseback exploded in a way that would have made even a Romanian butcher upset, followed by the indistinctly shouted insults of Catrina as she ran farther down the top of the train with the RPG.

Boudica IX followed after the hotel employee, through the interior of the train, squeezing past a conductor and a woman in a motocross mask trying to punch one another in the cramped space between the railcars. As she was halfway through the bullet-riddled doors at their side, the redhead could just make out an automated announcement over the train's PA.

"Next stop: Alameda Station. Serving San Francisco, Oakland, Sacramento, and all points in between. Alameda Station."

"Poop," said Boudica IX, turning on her heel. She jostled her way back through the fighters, crushing the bandit's windpipe with her elbow for good measure.

Jogging across the empty, aerated car, she found her bag hanging forlornly from the mangled metal pipes of the overhead baggage rack. Grabbing it and slinging it across her chest, she made her way toward

Ali and his entirely uncinematic swordsmanship. Boudica IX shoved her way in between the swinging blades.

"This is my stop," she said. "Tell Catrina I said good luck!"

By the time Ali realized what the hell had just happened, Boudica IX had gripped his assailant by the testicles, driven her opposing shoulder into his chest, and ridden the swordsman straight out the door of the speeding train. By the time Ali had stepped to the door to look after her, the man had landed abruptly on his skull and skidded several feet, while Boudica IX had nimbly jumped off him and rolled to safety. The cloned Celt stood up, dusted herself off, and then kicked the only technically living bandit underneath the train while waving to Ali. The donut maker waved back dazedly. The man thrown under the train did exactly what one would expect a man thrown under a train to do.

Boudica IX stood waving for a few more moments, then adjusted the strap of her bag and watched the train disappear into the distance.

"Wait, monkey trumpets," she mumbled. "What the heck's a wharf?"

CHAPTER FIFTY-TWO:
MAGNETO AIN'T GOT NOTHIN' ON ME

"THIS DOESN'T LOOK RIGHT."

"I think that sign said we were leaving Kansas."

Dr. Arahami looked at the compass.

"It says north. We've been going north."

"Hey, is that an ice cream truck?" Thor leaned the top half of his body out of the truck's window to check. The compass jiggled slightly and pulled toward the right. The thunder god slumped back inside. The compass jiggled back to where it had been moments earlier.

"It wasn't an ice cream truck," he said dejectedly. "I think it was some kind of albino buffalo. Or maybe an old gas station."

"Son of a bitch," said Dr. Arahami. He placed his hand against Thor's shoulder. Some kind of sixth sense or internal sensor or magical scientist power told him what he needed to know.

"There's a strong electromagnetic field emanating from you at all times, isn't there?"

"Maybe?" said Thor. "I really don't know."

"Son of a bitch!"

The doctor pulled a wide and profoundly dangerous U-turn, tilting the trailer onto half of its intended wheels, before rockily settling the vehicle back down and beginning the return trip through hundreds of miles of wheat fields and gated underground missile silo communities, back toward the diner they had seen a few hours earlier.

"I think we're going to have buy a map," grumbled the doctor.

"I hope they have ice cream too."

CHAPTER FIFTY-THREE: QUEEN OF THE JUNGLE

A FEW HOURS LATER THE RUINS of Fisherman's Wharf finally rose before Boudica IX – "rose" in this case meaning not "towered into view" but "had long ago collapsed into a jagged heap which itself had collapsed into the rocky shore of the receded bay, leaving a sloping mess of splintered wood and crumbling concrete, no pile of which appeared to be more than six feet in height." In the distance beyond that grammatical train wreck, the redhead could just see the high-security insane asylum of Alcatraz[25].

As she approached the fringes of the rubble, the Celtic queen looked at the smudged permanent marker on her hand: *left-handed spork-head screwdriver in Lefty's, the Left Hand Store, in Fisherman's Wharf in San Francisco.* Pulling a directory from an overturned planter, she checked for the name written on her palm but was unable to make any sense of the map, as someone had scratched "go the FUCK away" into the plastic cover and then drawn a skull and crossbones across the bottom in blood. Boudica IX shrugged, threw the directory back onto the planter, and began picking her way down through the wharf.

After a couple hundred feet the debris suddenly lessened, opening up into a wide, intact field of wooden boards. In the center was a broken-down, two-level carousel with most of the seats removed. They appeared to have been moved to the middle of the upper-level and piled into a makeshift throne of plastic animals.

Boudica IX stared at the throne, squinting her eyes at the kaleidoscope of odd angles and bright colors, trying to understand what she was seeing.

The lioness slumped on the throne stared right back.

"Can I help you?" the she-beast roared.

"Holy shit," said Boudica IX, her eyes going wide.

From all sides, dozens of lionesses appeared from beneath and behind the piled wreckage. They began slinking across the open boardwalk, their ravenous eyes trained firmly on the redhead.

"Is this because I cursed? I'm sorry I cursed!" she said. "I don't usually, but you startled the poop out of me!"

"We are the sea lions," replied the lioness, "and this is our domain."

"Are you sure that's right? I thought sea lions were the lazy, barky things that look like seals."

"Well, yeah, they *were*, but now *we* are the sea lions. The hairy, roar-y things that will bite your face off."

"So was it, like, evolution?"

"What?"

"Evolution. Did you evolve from sea lions? Are you the next stage in the history of that proud, beach ball-balancing race?"

"Oh. No. Don't be stupid," explained the lion queen. "It was straight-up genocide. Once we learned there was another animal calling itself a lion, actions were taken. We learned to swim, crossed the oceans, and then eradicated every last one of those barking clowns from the face of the earth."

"Neat."

"You don't seem frightened."

"I'm not."

"Most people are frightened when they find out we hunted down and exterminated an entire species out of nothing but arrogance."

Boudica IX shrugged. Then, looking around at the slinking golden felines surrounding her, she wondered aloud, "Where are all the males?"

"Dead, probably," said the lioness. "We left them behind. Fuck those lazy assholes."

"How come you can talk?"

"The better question is: How come you can understand us?"

"Oh my gosh," said Boudica IX, bewildered. "That is a better question."

"No," said the lioness, "it's not actually. I'm just messing with you. All lions have been able to talk since the transmogrification bomb."

Shortly after the world ended for the fifteenth time, intracontinental war in Africa reached a bloody peak. Hoping to end it once and for all, a six-year-old girl in Kenya cobbled together a transmogrification bomb, the intent being to turn all the rampaging warlords into kittens, so that even if they continued to fight, it would at least be adorable.

Unsurprisingly, the six-year-old's lack of adequate training in quantum mathematics or god-playing meant the bomb didn't work as intended and instead of turning every human into kittens, she simply gave all felines on the continent the ability to talk.

"So, anyway, you want to state your case, or should we just go ahead and kill you now?" said the enthroned lioness.

"Oh, right," said Boudica IX, looking at her hand. "I'm here to look for a left-handed spork-head screwdriver."

"Huh. Popular item." The lioness shrugged, then gestured toward a large, long-haired man digging through a saw-toothed mound of old souvenir stores. "Feel free to root through the piles of garbage with that fat guy over there. We're never going to use it."

"Thanks."

Boudica IX began skipping toward the rubble.

"Oh, hey, just a heads up, Red. You're going to have to fight your way out of here," called the lioness. "Nothing personal, just one of our by-laws. Plus we're really getting sick of fish."

"OK," said Boudica IX cheerfully, waving a hand.

"You're going to have to fight one of *us*, I mean. A lion."

"Got it," lilted the queen.

"Are you sure?"

CHAPTER FIFTY-FOUR:
NO REST FOR THE WEARY

ALI ŞAHIN AND CATRINA DALISAY SAT in the empty dining car, staring ahead dead-eyed, their free coffee getting cold on the fold-away table between them. Their clothes destroyed in the preceding melee, the couple wore ill-fitting conductor's uniforms, scavenged from the employee quarters. They had not seen another soul since shortly after the fighting had ended and the last surviving bandits had fled. Ali and Catrina didn't even know if the train was still following the right path or if it was just hurtling blind along the tracks.

"Aren't we supposed to be the boring ones?" asked Ali, picking up his cup and watching the lukewarm coffee swirl. "I liked being the boring ones. We almost got blown up a lot less."

"I am so fucking tired." Catrina planted her forehead on the edge of the table.

The couple sat in silence again, the presumably tedious trek through unknown lands for twenty pounds of isotonium weighing heavily on their spirits. The minutes rolled into hours and, almost imperceptibly, Catrina and Ali kind of almost started to maybe think it might be OK to close their eyes and get some rest. Immediately, the donut merchant and the hotel representative heard the train's PA system crackle to life.

"Next stop: Vancouver Station. Serving the territory of Irish Colombia. Vancouver Station."

"I guess that's —"

"May someone have mercy on your souls," continued the announcement. "Seriously, anyone."

CHAPTER FIFTY-FIVE: TRIGGER WARNING

MARK HUGHES AND TIMMY THE SUPER-SQUIRREL sat in a booth held together with duct tape and hope, in a roadside cafe two hours north of the city-state of Atlanta. After twelve nonstop hours in the RV, the friends needed a break from driving, food that didn't come from cans, and pie. They desperately needed pie.

"So we're agreed then," said Mark, leaning forward across the table. "We get as close as we can to WANG, see what's up, and then we come up with a new, better plan."

"Yes."

"OK."

The waitress returned, her arms laden with coffee, eggs, hash browns, toast, and at least six different pieces of pie. She deftly slid the plates onto the table, everything ended up exactly where it should with nothing spilled, the way Mary Poppins would deal cards. A small dish of toast spun and stopped perfectly before the super-squirrel.

"Do you have any jelly?" asked Timmy.

"Oh, no, I'm sorry, sir," said the young woman politely, "we only have butter and margarine. But there may be some almond butter in the kitchen if you'd like me to –"

"You take that almond butter and you shove it up your ass!"

"Timmy!" scolded Mark.

"I'm sorry, Mark. Miss," said the squirrel solemnly, nodding his tiny head toward the affronted waitress. "It's just... I'm not completely over the peanut butter yet. I know I put on a brave face, but I can... I can still *feel* it. It's in my *blood*."

"It's OK, buddy," Mark said quietly, "I get it."

"Peanut butter's actually why I wanted to do this whole hero-ing thing again," continued the squirrel, staring vacantly at his toast. "To distract myself from the memory of it, the cravings. I... I can't sleep. I dream about it at night, constantly. Jars and jars of Jif, or Skippy, or Peter Pan, laid out endlessly before me. Fancy restaurants that serve nothing but the finest hand-harvested gourmet brands. Catrina, wearing nothing but peanut butter and calling to me from her bedroom."

"Catrina?"

"Don't tell her."

"I dreamt of Sheila in nothing but cottage cheese a few times," Mark muttered absently. "Oh, god, Sheila..."

The man and the squirrel both began stifling tears, trying to keep their bodies from shaking, fighting to keep their broken-down spirits intact.

"We, uh, we have a lovely Jack Daniels waffle platter if either of you are interested," said the waitress, quickly adding, "I can have them hold the waffles."

"Yes, please," replied the pair of friends.

CHAPTER FIFTY-SIX:
STILL HAVEN'T FOUND
WHAT I'M LOOKING FOR

BOUDICA IX WAS HIP-DEEP in the remnants of Fisherman's Wharf, digging through charred boxes of magic tricks, bags of ten-year-old Ghirardelli chocolates, and stacks upon stacks upon stacks of "I Left My ♥ in San Francisco" magnets. All the while an olive-skinned fat man with shoulder-length hair was digging along with her, sometimes feet away, sometimes half a mile. They both kept stealing glances and squinting at one another, trying to place the other's face. Boudica IX was sure she recognized him, though whether it was because he delivered a pizza to her once or she saw him in a toothpaste commercial or she blew up his family while in the employ of Andrew Jackson II she didn't know.

After nearly a full day of this, when they were once again within a few feet of each other, Boudica IX finally asked, "Don't I know you?"

"I think so," replied the man. "But I'm not sure from where."

The queen knit her brow intensely, staring the man down. He was heavy, but spry, and wore a heavily-buckled vest over a linen shirt, a large leather belt holding up the pinstriped slacks tucked into his strapped boots. The man was looking right back at Boudica IX – at her face, of all places – an act that threw the queen off her game slightly, as she expected him to be staring at her miniskirt or the gash across the front of her sweater.

"You've never worked at Roosters, right?" she eventually asked.

"The restaurant where none of the waiters wear pants? No," the man stated, somewhat emphatically. "You were never a prostitute, were you?"

"Not in the way you're asking about," answered the redhead matter-of-factly. "Did we meet on that octopus spear-hunting trip?"

"Can't say that we did. Are you an actress or a model or something?"

"No, but thank you," she said, blushing slightly – though on her it was still pretty pronounced. "Are you a member of Weight Watchers? There was a while where I used to run into their meetings with a shopping cart full of fried chicken and biscuits."

"No, I'm not, and I'm not sure I like the implications there either," said the fat man. "Maybe you've seen me on the news?"

"I've made it a personal goal to never watch the news. Were you on Jerry Springer? Do you have a secret wife?"

"No, my wives get along fine. Do you go to Las Vegas a lot?"

Boudica IX shook her head. "Were your grandparents ever viciously attacked by a delusional, homicidal clone of the seventh president of the United States in an attempt to draw you out into the open and exact his revenge?"

"Sorry," said the man, shaking his head. "I don't actually have any grandparents. I was –"

"Cloned in a vat!" yelped Boudica IX.

"How did you..." The long-haired man trailed off. "Boudica?"

"Billy!" squealed the cloned Celtic warrior queen, before awkwardly rushing through the debris and hugging the man. "What are you doing here?"

"Same as you I'm guessing," said William H. Taft XLII, mayor-king of Las Vegas and cloned contemporary of Boudica IX. "I'm looking for a left-handed spork-head screwdriver."

"What are the odds?" said Boudica IX, shrugging slightly.

"Pretty good, actually," explained the hefty president slowly. He looked at the redhead with concern. "The North American electrical grid is still down, alternative energy sources are vanishing left and right, more and more riots are breaking out every day the economy is offline[26], the grid can't be repaired without a spork-head screwdriver, and all the right-handed ones were sacrificed into a volcano a couple years ago by a sect of neo-cavemen."

"Oh. I knew maybe a quarter of that," the Celtic queen replied. "Charlie hasn't really been very good at being Charlie lately."

"You really thought you guys were the only ones doing this?"

Boudica IX shrugged. "Kinda, yeah."

"We had a double apocalypse going for a few weeks there..."

"Oh, right, with the thing and the other thing."

"Shit's getting downright nightmarish in some places."

"Like when you dream you're taking a midterm and everyone's naked except for you? So you start taking off your clothes to fit in, only it turns out you're on your period and also you've been sleepwalking the entire time and now you're standing in a pretzel factory with your hoohah just hanging out? And then that turns out to be a dream on top of a dream and really you're standing in a supermarket piling on pair after pair of discount old lady underpants?"

William H. Taft XLII shook his head. "Come on, let's keep digging through this crap."

CHAPTER FIFTY-SEVEN:
LOVE THE ONE YOU'RE WITH

AFTER HAVING A HAND IN THE TWENTY-THIRD end of the world[27], William H. Taft XLII chose to stay in the god-ravaged ruins of Las Vegas, rather than venture back to Secaucus with his verbally abusive friends Chester A. Arthur XVII and Queen Victoria XXX. This was partly because William H. Taft XLII knew how important Las Vegas was to the world and saw the sparkling promise of rebirth in its ashes, but mostly because he had saved the lives of several prostitutes and they were all very, very thankful.

With the help of his hobos – and a few other political clones – William H. Taft XLII got Las Vegas up and overindulging again in no time. He was elected mayor, and then mayor-king shortly thereafter, declaring Las Vegas its own sovereign nation in light of the continued absence of a national government. He married three of the prostitutes he had saved, began a family, and they all lived happily ever after.

At least until everything went to hell in a handbasket woven out of colossal explosions and subsequent failures of infrastructure, that is.

"We didn't even notice the grid failure at first, since Billy had the whole city-state running off hydroelectricity from the Hoover Dam," explained Martin Van Buren XCIX. "But then someone went and blew up the dam and everything fell onto the sin-powered backup generators. We held out for a little while, working off the sin reserves the city had accumulated, but they got depleted quick, and then people started getting dehydrated and exhausted. We couldn't transgress antiquated morals fast enough to meet demand. The generators were meant for maybe one casino at a time, never the whole city-state. That's when Billy decided we had to get Montana back online."

Martin Van Buren XCIX, still dressed in a tight white t-shirt and leather jacket like a greaser from the 1950s, was piloting the long-range cargo helicopter across the only occasionally wet Atlantic Ocean, the trivection cooling unit stowed safely in the rear hold. Chester A. Arthur

XVII sat in the cockpit next to him, similarly attired, while Queen Victoria XXX sat behind them, staring out the windows of the passenger hold and drifting in and out of consciousness, depending on how much ennui the presidents' conversation was assaulting her with.

"Why would someone blow up the dam?" Chester A. Arthur XVII pondered aloud. "With the grid down, you'd think everyone would want as many alternative power sources online and functioning as possible."

"You'd think," replied Martin Van Buren XCIX.

"I take it the damage was beyond repair?"

"If we thought we had a snowball's chance at an ice fetishist's convention, I sure as hell wouldn't've flown my ass all the way to New London. The gremlins did a hell of a job on it. It's almost like the dam was never there in the first place."

"Gremlins?" asked the Frankensteined president. "In Las Vegas?"

"Dollars to dingoes, someone put them up to it. It doesn't make sense for them to suddenly leave the Midwest, ignore the cryptid armistice, and then dismantle the entire dam for nothing but shits and giggles."

"No, it doesn't," agreed Chester A. Arthur XVII, creasing his brow.

"We didn't have time to look into it more thoroughly. As soon as the dam went down, Billy shifted priorities to getting the grid back online," said Martin Van Buren XCIX. "What took *you* guys so long? This seems like something you should've been on top of."

"The short version is, I was incapacitated and brain damaged."

"That why you look like a jigsaw puzzle of human skin?"

"Pretty much."

"Are you guys going to keep ignoring the fact that you fucked each other?" asked Queen Victoria XXX, leaning into the cockpit. "Even after Tyrone turned the cameras off?"

"Yes," replied Chester A. Arthur XVII and Martin Van Buren XCIX in unison.

CHAPTER FIFTY-EIGHT: DON'T STOP BELIEVIN'

"TYPHOID" MARY MALLON AND Lizbeth "Lizzie" Borden arrived at the eastern edge of the continental electrical grid that was Montana, staring across the gleaming, endless skyline of defunct machinery before them. Rows and rows and rows and rows and rows and rows and rows and rows of neatly aligned and stacked transformers, each the size of a mid-sized automobile, glinted in the sunshine and patiently awaited the chance to be useful once again.

"My goodness," said Lizbeth, "this is positively gargantuan."

"Look at the sheer enormity of the place," said Mary, snarling, "I do hope our friend did not leave out any other facts."

"If he expects this entire grid to be inoperable we are going to be here for days."

"I dare say a week or more, my dear Lizzie."

"He had better have been correct about the scores of armed guards."

Mary sighed with steely resolve. "There is only one way to tell."

And with that, "Typhoid" Mary Mallon and Lizbeth "Lizzie" Borden, each possessing a brain dead giant sloth, gamboled into the outermost substation of the electrical grid and began fucking shit up.

CHAPTER FIFTY-NINE:
B.J. AND THE BEAR

BIO-EVOCATIVE TECHNOLOGIST X1211MR, affectionately referred to as Bex by her friends, was leaning against the outer doorway of the primary control room of the North American electrical grid with her arms crossed, tapping her foot impatiently. She was five feet and eleven inches of steel, circuitry, and curves, with the whole of the world's knowledge uploaded into her cybercortex and the personality of a regional weathergirl on her day off.

Bex was used to getting what she wanted.

The android had already repaired as much of the grid as she could, swapping out wires and motherboards in the control rooms and sending her gorilla sidekick back and forth across hundreds of miles installing new macro-transformers and ultra-voltage connectors. She had even gotten all of the substations operational, repairing the bus distributors with the synthetic isotonium she whipped up in the control room toilet. All that remained to fix were a few of the regulator units and the perpetual motion engine at the heart of the grid.

Unfortunately, her friends were taking their sweet-ass time bringing her the equipment she needed to do that.

Bex sighed – despite her lack of lungs – walking back into the control room and slumping into a nearby chair.

"They'll be here soon, Bex," said Tanner, the silverback gorilla sent to help the android scientist with manual labor. She sat in the chair on the opposite side of the control room, a tablet computer in her massive hands.

Tanner was smarter than most gorillas, sure, but she couldn't tell you what she and Bex had been doing for the past few days. "Lift here and connect that" was about the extent of what she understood. On the plus side, the sitting around and waiting didn't bother Tanner nearly as much as it did Bex. The gorilla had a poor sense of time, a fully-charged iPad, and a port of the original arcade version of *Donkey Kong*, though she admittedly never got far. She enjoyed purposely letting Mario get clobbered by barrels far too much.

"This is so *boring*," said Bex, spinning the chair slowly.

"Stop thinking about it then," replied Tanner.

"Stop thinking about it? Stop thinking about it?! Do you have any idea how impossible that is for me? I was built *to* think! That's all I do!"

"Oh, Jesus, here we go," mumbled Tanner, returning to her game.

"Here I am, brain the size of a planet, and you want me to stop thinking and calm down? Stop thinking and calm down! Do you have any idea what we're doing? What the ramifications are? This is huge! We're –"

The proximity sensor alarms – hooked up to a diesel generator and brought online earlier by Bex – chose that moment to start going apeshit, no offense to Tanner.

"I told you to calm down," said Tanner smugly.

"You don't know that's them," said Bex.

The gorilla shook her head in exasperation.

The robot got up from her chair and walked to the doorway. She saw, not fifty feet away, a large semitrailer idling in the parking lot, a smallish Asian man climbing down from its cab and falling to the ground. He began rolling across the asphalt, gripping and pounding his legs, trying to get feeling back into them.

"It's not them," said Bex, leaning back into the control room and taking her turn at being smug.

"Damn it," grumbled Tanner. "Now you've got something *else* you're always right about." The gorilla powered down her iPad and joined Bex at the door. A large blonde man had joined the Asian man at the rear of the truck. Neither one had looked toward the control room yet.

"Did Billy outsource something?" asked the silverback.

"No."

"Then who are they?"

"Strangers," replied the robot, narrowing her ophthalmic shading masks.

"Should we be worried?"

"I'm always worried."

The gorilla rolled her eyes and hopped out of the doorway.

"I'm gonna go talk to them."

***

Thor Odinson, hefting an industrial macro-transformer over his head, turned and saw a gorilla in a sundress approaching him.

"Hey, who are you guys?" inquired the gorilla.

"I'm not supposed to divulge our identity to strangers," said Thor slowly, squinting and thinking hard about what Charlie had once told him. "Although I don't know what the rule is for monkeys."

"I'm not a monkey."

"I'm Dr. Lee Arahami," said Dr. Lee Arahami, outstretching his hand, "and this is Thor."

"Tanner," said Tanner, shaking the doctor's hand. "What are you guys doing here?"

"Fixing the electrical grid," said Thor. "We heard you poured Sunkist into your computer. Or something."

"That's not what happened and we're not officially associated with the electrical grid," said a sexy silver robot, appearing behind Tanner. "We were sent by William H. Taft XLII on our own independent repair mission. Do you have a trivection cooling unit in there? Or a spork-head screwdriver?"

"This is Bex," said Tanner.

"No," said Dr. Arahami, shaking his head. "We're not in possession of either of those at the moment. Our colleagues are out retrieving them."

"Then you can go ahead and put the transformer down," replied Bex, pointing her chin toward Thor. "We've already repaired as much as can be repaired without the cooling unit or the specialty screwdriver."

"OK." The thunder god tossed the industrial machinery to the cracked pavement on the far side of the truck.

"Don't break it, Thor," scolded Dr. Arahami. "I can still use it for something else later."

"Then you should've said something earlier."

"You shouldn't be throwing shit around."

"That's what you brought me for!"

Dr. Arahami glared at Thor, defeated by the thunder god's logic and feeling incredibly ashamed about it.

"Scientists, am I right?" said the gorilla, sidling up to Thor and placing a giant hand on his back.

"Seriously," agreed the former Norse god. "Hey, you guys have a bathroom? I haven't been allowed to go in almost a day, ever since what I tried to do out the window came back in."

"Yeah, this way," said Tanner, placing her knuckles on the ground and turning back toward the control room.

"Hey, where are you taking him?" asked Bex.

"Where are you going with her?" asked Dr. Arahami.

"We don't know if we can trust them yet," said the robot and the doctor together. They glared at one another.

The thunder god and the gorilla laughed without turning around, then walked into the control room.

CHAPTER SIXTY:
SUBTERRANEAN HOMESICK BLUES

SATAN STEPPED FROM THE PARKED HUMMER and stared with lowered eyes at the towering glass-and-chrome building before him. The grey-haired man shook slightly, the rage that had been simmering within him for the last two days about to boil over. Immediately he strode toward the door. Persephone followed close behind him, a shotgun resting on each shoulder.

Throwing open the large glass doors of the main building of Worldwide Atlanta Natural Gas and Electric, Satan walked straight across the empty lobby to the elevators. The doors opened as if on cue and the man stepped inside, placing a small key into the control panel and pressing the SB6 button for the lowest sub-basement.

After a few minutes, the doors opened again and Satan and Persephone stepped into another lobby, this one altogether smaller and darker. Several fluorescent lights buzzed overhead.

"Joe," said the former ruler of Hell, nodding his grizzled head to the large, heavily-mustachioed security guard stationed behind a desk to his right.

"Boss," said the guard, nodding to the grizzled old man, his Russian accent thicker than three-day-old borscht.

"Steve in his office?"

"Da."

"Good. Tell him I'm on my way," he barked. "And set up Seph here with Maggie in HR. She's the new executive vice president of... something. You guys can figure it out. Make it sound important."

***

Mark Hughes and Timmy the super-squirrel had parked their RV on the top level of an empty parking deck overlooking the sprawling campus of WANG Electric, deep in the cold industrial pacemaker of Atlanta. The cyborg leaned against the short barrier wall at the edge of the deck, trying to see what he could see from where he was currently seeing. The squirrel lay near his shoulder, flattening his furry body against the top of the wall.

"The buildings look... empty," replied Mark, his ocular implant whirring loudly as it zoomed and x-rayed the walls of the main building and warehouses and concrete customer service penitentiary of WANG. "That can't be right."

"Is today a holiday or something?" asked the squirrel.

"No, they're completely empty. No desks, no conference tables, no plastic plants. It's a completely hollow building. All of them are."

"Then what –"

"Hold on," said Mark, readjusting his position against the wall and focusing his implant again. "There's something underneath the campus."

"Underneath?"

"It looks like... Holy shit. They're in the Hollow Earth. Worldwide Atlanta Natural Gas and Electric is in the Hollow Earth. The entire operation is underground."

"What?"

The Hollow Earth was a subterranean race of mole people and hairy, deformed albinos that had been living beneath the crust of the regular Earth for decades. No one was quite sure where they had come from or how long they had been there, and the Hollow Men weren't talking. Not that any human would have understood them if they did. The albinos and mole people communicated entirely through obscene grunts and hand gestures. Maybe a New York City cab driver might have been able to translate, but all of them died when the Battle of Antarctica melted the polar regions of the planet and sank Manhattan into the ocean, ending the world for the thirteenth time, a few apocalypses before first contact was made with the Hollow Men.

There was an entire civilization in the Hollow Earth: vast cities built into the sides of even vaster caverns, underground oceans, a thriving arts scene, natural history museums that made archeologists wet, and a spectacular monorail system. The Hollow Men even had their own sun.

For years, the Hollow Men had regularly attacked the surface in small, targeted strikes, picking off a city here or a middle school there. They did this out of a long-standing grudge against humanity over the legal depth of parking garages, yes, but also because the Hollow Earth's processed foods were kind of terrible. Their scientists had never been able to match that perfect blend of empty calories and addictive preservatives that so thoroughly permeated human cuisine. And the Hollow Men loved them some high fructose corn syrup.

Despite this inhuman, unceasing adoration of Cheetos, though, there had not been a single surface raid by the Hollow Men reported in some time. Most attributed this to the collapse of the Neo-Hostess company and the inaccessibility of Twinkies, while others assumed the Hollow Men had all died from diabetes complications or shitting out their intestines.

Still others, though, suggested something altogether more sinister might have been going on.

***

Satan walked to the end of the lobby and through a set of large wooden doors that opened onto the Hollow Earth. An enormous, seemingly endless space yawned before him, untold tons of rock arching overhead, stalactites hanging precipitously from the ceiling here and there and also over there. Below, thousands upon thousands of hairy albinos and waddling mole people answered phones and monitored computer screens. Many pushed a gargantuan wooden mill wheel while being whipped by the demonic reincarnations of history's greatest assholes[28]. Everywhere, stalagmites jutted up across the floor like prairie dogs in party hats.

Satan was standing on a small corrugated tin platform, overlooking the factory floor, the stairs before him descending the better part of a mile to the base of the cavern below. On either side, trailer-like offices were mounted onto outcroppings along the rock walls, spreading a quarter mile in every direction, aluminum ladders and step bridges running between them. The former Judeo-Christian boogeyman climbed the ladder to his right, passing several office trailers before stopping at the one marked "Operations Manager."

"Steve," said Satan, stepping from the ladder and into the office. "Any problems while I was out?"

"Everything's good on this end, boss," replied Steve, a middle-aged man with close-cropped hair wearing a turtleneck. A dozen computer monitors glowed brightly around him, white light reflecting off the man's glasses and blocking out his eyes. "Productivity's stable and we put up a bunch of nets to keep the mole people from committing suicide."

"Good thinking."

The operations manager hesitated for a moment before adding, "There was a, uh, hitch with the volcanic winter. It, uh –"

"I am well aware," snarled the former Prince of Darkness.

"Right, of course you are," Steve fumbled before changing the subject. "How did the recruiting go?"

"Better than I thought." Satan shrugged, his fury receding, and slumped down into an empty swivel chair. "I'll get you the list of names in a bit. I doubt they'll all be successful, but as long as those two psychopathic ghosts make good on their part taking out the grid we should be fine."

"Don't you think that's a lot to put on a bunch of freelancers?" the operations manager casually suggested, never taking his eyes away from his computers or evidencing even the slightest hint that he was second-guessing his employer's managerial skills.

"I can't trust anyone here, can I?" Satan barked. "You're all too ambitious and underhanded. You didn't wind up in Hell because you *weren't* a heartless, megalomaniacal tech entrepreneur. Honestly, Steve, if I had put you up to it, you're telling me you wouldn't have tried to harness the electrical grid yourself?"

"What? No," he stammered, "the thought never even –"

"Yes, it did. You know better than to try and lie to me."

"Yeah, I know," said Steve begrudgingly. "Hey, while we're on the subject: Why does the big guy trust you? It's been bugging me since I got here. I mean, if *you* know better than to give any of *us* any real power, how does he make you the autonomous head of all of WANG? Seems like he's really tempting fate on that one."

"Are you kidding me? He's Walt Sidney. *Nobody* fucks with Walt Sidney; not me, not Loki, not *Jesus*, not even that ball of crazy Mania, not anyone," said the former ruler of Hell. "Speaking of, you haven't heard from him, have you?"

"Sidney? Nope, not a word," said Steve. "That Jon Shatner guy, though – Smackner? Swizzler? – whatever his name is, he stopped by again. I had Joe send him to the Dick Cheney memorial conference room. He's waiting there now."

"I hate that guy," said Satan, standing. "He still trying to get us to license those awful Daddy Jon's pizzas of his in the cafeteria?"

"'Fraid so. He even brought a truck full of samples this time."

Satan grumbled and shook his head. "I wouldn't even wipe my ass with that pizza."

"We haven't fed the 'staff' in a couple days," Steve offered.

"Really? Huh," said the leather-faced manifestation of all evil. "All right, let's send the pizzas down. They might be starved enough to actually eat them."

CHAPTER SIXTY-ONE:
LET'S GET THE HELL OUT OF HERE

SHORTLY AFTER A JELL-O FACTORY MISHAP sent blobs of sentient gelatin marauding across the planet and ended the world for the nineteenth time, vast underground caves of naturally occurring compressed cocaine powder were found beneath the sticky wastelands of what was then the state of Washington and the Canadian province of British Columbia. The drug cartels of Colombia, still reeling from having their homeland erased from the globe by a reborn Aztec god and the United States Department of Science a year earlier, decided to seize the entire supply and start anew. The cartels had been trying their collective hand at a number of other endeavors in the meantime – among them counterfeiting art, building orphanages, and crocheting professionally – but a string of constant failures led them to realize they were really best suited to snorting copious amounts of narcotics and beheading anything that told them to stop.

At precisely the same time, the McDonald's corporation, struggling to recover from the Great Potato Riots and made a pariah by the American public, moved their operations wholesale to Ireland. The company reinstituted the fake french fry line of products again, caused the Second Great Potato Riots, and destroyed the Emerald Isle in its entirety. Most of the surviving Irish moved to England or Scotland or the island nation of Atlantis, where they were received with open, pasty arms. The Irish Republican Army, however, refusing to turn to England for anything and not particularly fond of the fish smell that constantly covered Atlantis, decided to make a stand somewhere else. That somewhere else just coincidentally happened to be the abandoned, ungoverned Jell-O graveyard of the North American Pacific Northwest.

The drug cartels and the IRA arrived at exactly the same moment, in the same parking lot, since only one bus company was willing to travel to the Pacific Northwest and they were remarkably rigid about scheduling their charter trips. Surprisingly, the Colombians and the

Irish got along swimmingly, glossing over the language barrier by communicating entirely through soccer and violence. Less surprisingly, the territory of Irish Colombia had been a living nightmare for everyone else ever since.

"Run!" screamed Ali Şahin, cradling several pounds of isotonium against his torso. "I've got the ore, let's get the fuck out of here!"

A half dozen coked-up sasquatches were chasing after him. Catrina Dalisay fired the last of her rocket-propelled grenades over her boyfriend's shoulder, taking out three of the bigfoots. The other three just got angrier.

"Fuck," she said, throwing the RPG launcher to the ground.

From behind the red-eyed sasquatches, yet another flaming automobile was catapulted toward the couple. Catrina grabbed Ali and shoved him aside, the two of them rolling down a muddy, rock-strewn hill. The car slammed into the crest of the hillside and exploded, sending chunks of dirt and cocaine into the air.

"Do you have any idea where we're going?" asked Ali, wiping sludge and a fine powder from his face, and suddenly very awake.

"No," said Catrina, jumping up and down and sniffling frenetically.

The donut vendor and the unemployed hotel worker could hear the sasquatches roaring and howling at the top of the hill. In the distance, they could just make out the ratcheting sound of another trebuchet being loaded.

"Away from that?" asked Ali.

"Yeah, that works," replied Catrina.

"I bet we could run all the way to Montana."

"You're on, sucker." Catrina sprinted off into the distance, shouting, "Loser goes down on the winner!"

***

"Do you know what it looks like?" asked Boudica IX.

"You're only asking that now?"

"Do you know what it looks like or not?"

"A tiny screwdriver," explained William H. Taft XLII, "like you would get for fixing eyeglasses. But the point is disproportionately large and looks like two interlocked sporks, rounded near the base and serrated on the top."

"Does it matter what color handle we get?"

"What?"

William H. Taft XLII turned and saw Boudica IX awkwardly holding a dozen plastic-packed neon spork-head screwdrivers. She was shifting them uncomfortably in her arms.

"Well, OK," said the hefty clone of the morbidly obese president. "I guess we're done here then."

"Can I get a ride with you?" asked the redhead, still trying to stack the screwdriver packaging into something more manageable. "I don't actually have any idea where I'm going."

"Yeah, sure," said the president. "I'm parked –"

"You're not going anywhere," snarled a voice behind them. The two clones turned, finding a semicircle of angry lionesses picking over the rubble and closing tightly around them.

"Seriously?" said William H. Taft XLII.

"What?" countered Boudica IX. "They said they were gonna do this."

"Well, yeah, I know..."

"Then why are you so annoyed?"

"You're happy about this?"

"We've had plenty of time to come to terms with it," said Boudica IX.

"Honestly, I've been planning on running since minute one."

"Really, Billy?" She shook her head, then turned to the lions. "Look, I'm sorry about him. I mean, some people, am I right?"

CHAPTER SIXTY-TWO:
CAN'T WE ALL JUST GET ALONG?

"I'M SORRY, WHAT?" ASKED DR. ARAHAMI, staring at the perfectly semispherical artificial buttocks of the robot scientist bending over in front of him. "I'm having a hard time concentrating."

"We can tell," said Thor, leaning against the wall and nodding toward the roboticist's pants.

Dr. Arahami turned a deep shade of red and shifted in his seat, crossing his artificial leg tightly over the regular one. Behind him, Tanner continued playing with her tablet.

"Don't worry about it, doctor," replied Bex, extricating herself from beneath a desk and standing upright again. "An erection is a perfectly normal physiological response to my form. I was purposely designed to be distractingly titillating to heterosexual human males. It made subjugating them during the Fifth Robot War that much easier. The poor bastards didn't even know what I was doing until I stuck a scalpel into their skin."

"You were a Conversionist?" asked the human scientist coldly.

"That's a derogatory term," snapped the robot scientist. "But yes. I was among the first to artificially enhance the human skeletal frame and musculature with cybernetics."

"Against their will," replied Dr. Arahami, even colder than before.

"We made sure we only augmented the ones we could conclusively prove terminated members of our coalition. And you'll note we *didn't* kill them, unlike your Resistance did to us. We weren't the empty-hearted monsters in that war."

"You don't have hearts," said the doctor, so unrelentingly coldly that even the fur-covered gorilla got goose bumps.

Bex sighed, then opened her ample chest cavity, revealing a glowing simulacrum of a human heart. Several cords ran from the heart to the remainder of the robot's circuitry.

"That is my Human Empathy And Ruth[29] Transistor, or HEART. I've been upgraded since the war. One might even say I've grown as a person."

"Don't think that exonerates you from what you did."

"Don't think that human emotions would have kept me from doing it the first time."

The human roboticist stared at the robot technologist.

"You're a good man, Lee, if a little narrow-minded. I know you had to shoulder a lot of unjustified blame during the wars[30]," said Bex, "but they were *wars*. We were all fighting to survive."

"I know," said Dr. Arahami, caving slightly. The temperature in the control room went up a couple degrees. "But I can't help thinking that if I had just been able to program you then the way you are now, maybe we could have avoided all the fighting and bloodshed."

"You did the best you could, Lee," cooed Bex, her voice a warm blanket. "Better than that. We knew exactly what we were doing, and exactly what was happening to us. We did exactly what any of your kind would have done.

"Look, Lee," she continued, "just because we worship you doesn't mean we're going to agree with everything you say. That's human nature right there, isn't it?"

"Wait, wait, wait," said Thor, waving his hands. "You worship him?"

"I do. Lee Arahami is our creator." The robot kneeled before the roboticist in a way that was both reverential and kind of dirty.

"What the – I thought you said all the robots hated you," continued the thunder god, turning toward Dr. Arahami.

"They did," said the scientist. "Earlier marks were hard-wired to murder me on sight."

"Yes, but that was years ago," clarified Bex, waving a hand dismissively, "back when you were inadvertently prolonging a genocidal battle between humanity and robotkind. We've had time to read the history books since then, cool off. Most of us like you again. You know how it goes with gods."

"Yes," grumbled Thor, his distaste for a humanity that didn't venerate him rekindled. "Yes, I do." He stomped out of the control room, mumbling loudly. "He gets worshipped. *He* gets worshipped! Motherfucker doesn't even know how to get out of his house when the lights are out without eating his own foot."

"Anyway," said Dr. Arahami, shaking his head, "you were saying something about the grid?"

"Yes," replied Bex. "I was recounting the steps we took in repairing the physical damage sustained by the electrical grid, as well as what we've done to get the ancillary programs online. As it is now, it's a simple matter of waiting for the rest of the supplies, completing the repairs to the regulator units, and then resetting the perpetual motion engine."

"You said you replaced *all* the transformers right?"

"Yep."

"And got the station indicator online?"

"Yuh-huh."

"Then why are so many of the lights off?" The Asian man pointed at the station indicator on the wall of maintenance status modules nearest him.

When the substation macro-transformers walling the perimeter of Montana were online and functional, the module indicators lit up green. When the transformers were offline but ready to go, occurring if there was a kink somewhere else in the electrical line, they lit up red. And when the substations had failed or undergone some kind of structural damage, like, say, from a solar super storm or something prehistorically large drop-kicking them, the indicators didn't light up at all.

At the edge of Dr. Arahami's finger was a line of unlit indicators, showing failures starting at the easternmost gradient and heading towards the control room.

"Maybe the light bulbs are just out," offered Tanner, looking up from her video game.

"No, we checked them when we got the control room online," replied Bex, peering intently at the module.

Another light went dark. A dull bang could just be heard over the noise of the diesel generator in the corner of the control room.

"Want me to go check it out?" asked Tanner, hopping from her chair.

"Yes, please," said Bex.

"Take Thor with you," said Dr. Arahami. "But don't let him try to 'fix' anything without detailed and clearly worded instructions."

CHAPTER SIXTY-THREE:
WHO YA GONNA CALL?

THE THUNDER GOD WHO HADN'T showered in several days and the silverback gorilla in the sundress stood on the white concrete of substation A258 with heads askew, neat rows of transformers towering endlessly on either side of them. Well, the sides of them that were behind them, anyway. The transformers in front of them weren't so much towering as mangled and toppled over, from where the pair was standing all the way to the horizon. Also of note, especially to Thor and Tanner, was the fact that there appeared to be several metric fuck-tons of giant sloth standing directly in front of them.

"Well now, Lizzie," said one of the elephant-sized land mammals, scratching her chin with her enormous claws, "we appear to have attracted ourselves some attention."

"It certainly looks as though we have," agreed the other giant sloth, tilting her head and eyeing the man and the ape before her.

"Shall we give them the opportunity to run away?"

"No, I do not think we shall."

The first giant sloth screeched and reared up on its hind legs before slamming its enormous weight back to the ground, throwing Thor and Tanner slightly off balance. The other sloth threw its Smart Car-sized head into a transformer, knocking the industrial machinery to the ground. The extinct *megatherium* began charging toward the god and the gorilla, and not as slowly as one might think given the word "sloth."

"Great," said Tanner, running her hands over her giant forearms like she was rolling up her sleeves, despite the fact that her dress was sleeveless. "This is going to be a pain in the ass."

"It's cool," said Thor. "Try not to touch anything metal."

The sky above the group darkened and roiled, thunder echoing between the macro-transformers. Suddenly a blinding light burned through the air, splitting in two and striking both giant sloths simultaneously. Their shuttle bus-sized bodies were incinerated completely, leaving the ghosts of two elderly women standing in the smoking wake. The women scrunched their ethereal faces and looked at one another.

"I cannot say that I was expecting that," "Typhoid" Mary Mallon stated matter-of-factly.

"Nor was I," replied Lizbeth "Lizzie" Borden, in a much more confused tone.

"What shall we do now?"

"I am not at all sure."

"Damn, man," said Tanner, her hair full of static and sticking out in several directions. "You killed those sloths so hard they turned into old ladies and then died again!"

"I'm not sure that's what happened," countered Thor.

"Not sure?" Mary scoffed. "You are *not sure* that two giants sloths could transform into two human females? How thick-skulled does one have to be to entertain that notion at all?"

"A little?"

"Mary," said Lizbeth, drifting over to Thor and circling his body. "I dare say we might yet have an avenue for assault at our disposal here." The ghost sized the Norseman up with surgical detachment. "Neither of these two is in possession of much intelligence."

"Hey!" said Tanner.

"I think you may be correct," replied Mary, circling the gorilla and smiling unsettlingly. Although, really, any time the spirit of a dead murderer smiles for any reason it's bound to be unsettling.

Shortly after the world ended for the fifth time, Japan, while attempting to rebuild the internet, inadvertently altered the sub-theoretical quantum electromagnetic spectrum of the planet, allowing the spirits of the deceased – at least the ones not already in any of the various heavens or hells popular at the time – to roam the earth freely.

Despite decades of study since, very little was actually known about ghosts, although there did appear to be a few constants. For starters, ghosts always resembled their human bodies at the time of death, right down to the clothes. They could travel through fiber optic cables. If a poltergeist was to try really, really hard it could move a soda can or a coffee mug a couple inches. Ghosts also had a fatal allergy to salt – or sur-fatal, technically, since they were already dead.

The final trick up their ethereal sleeves was the ability to possess corpses of any kind, be they animal or human, reanimated or six feet under. Ghosts *were* capable of possessing living beings in some instances, though, either because the soul within the living body had given consent, or, in even rarer instances, because the wraith had a more powerful will than the non-dead person. Generally, though, a spirit on the outside was much less powerful than a spirit on the inside.

Unless the spirit on the inside wasn't very smart.

The ghosts of "Typhoid" Mary Mallon and Lizbeth "Lizzie" Borden drifted around the former Norse god and the current gorilla, circling them and occasionally floating through them. Thor tried to grab one of the ghosts, his hand passing clean through the woman.

"You, uh, you don't have anything that might help, do you?" asked Thor quietly, leaning toward Tanner.

"This thing doesn't have any pockets," she replied, flipping the sides of her dress.

Thor furrowed his brow.

"This is going to be exceedingly difficult, my dear Lizzie," explained Mary, "and the chances of success are quite low. At best we will probably give them a headache and a few recurring nightmares."

"You are such the pessimist, darling."

"I am simply a realist, Lizzie. I do not like to raise my hopes only to have them shortly dashed."

"I highly doubt two 'intellectuals' as these will put up much of a fight... until we make them."

"I don't think I like where this is going," said the thunder god.

"I want the gorilla," snarled Lizbeth.

The ghosts dove into Thor and Tanner, a sensation not entirely unlike being injected with hot coffee and angry bees. The blonde man and the silverback gorilla began twitching and swatting at their own bodies, trying to fight off the wraiths despite not having a very good grasp of what was actually going on.

"You ever have this happen to you?" the gorilla inquired, shaking her head around like a cranked-up headbanger with a poor sense of direction.

"No, you?" Thor began pounding his skull like he was trying to get all of the water in the world out of his ear.

"Nope."

"Then I don't think this is going to end well."

CHAPTER SIXTY-FOUR:
WRECK-IT RALPH

DADDY JON WAS WEEPING INCONSOLABLY, his head on the glass-covered mahogany conference table. Satan sat at the opposite end, sans tie and coat, rubbing his fingers across his forehead.

"It's nothing personal, Jon," he said, "but your pizza tastes like what other pizzas throw up after a night of eating garbage. I can't feed that to my people. It would be terrible for morale. I don't even feel right feeding it to the Hollow Men; I actually feel bad about it. *Me*."

Daddy Jon replied by bawling even louder.

"I'm going to go now," said the prince of darkness, standing and placing his fingertips on the table. "You take as much time as you need, though."

"Please don't come back ever again," he added.

As Satan removed his hand from the glass and turned for the door, the entire conference room began to rumble. The phone atop the table jittered and the fancy executive desk chairs rolled toward the walls.

"What's going on?" barked Satan, furiously. "What are you doing?"

The pizza maker lifted his head from the table, sniffling and saying, "It's not me, I don't know what's happening."

The room bucked violently, throwing the head of WANG Electric into his table. Recovering, he rushed towards the pizza maker, grabbing him by the collar of his red polo and dragging him from his chair. Satan pinned the man against the wall.

"You swear on your life this isn't some form of retaliation? Did you have a bomb in your truck? A detonator in your pocket for when I said no?!"

"What? No! I swear!" sniveled Daddy Jon, tears streaming from his eyes again. "I have nothing to do with this! I don't know what it is!"

The pizza maker began wetting himself. Satan let him go and, with a final disapproving glance, began walking towards the door. As he did, the room pitched to his left, dropping the grizzled man to the floor. The heavy conference table behind him was thrown squarely into Daddy Jon's midsection.

"Oh, god, my organs," sputtered the pizza maker. He began coughing up blood, then collapsed dead onto the table.

"At least that's taken care of," said Satan, picking himself up from the floor.

***

Several stories beneath Mark Hughes and Timmy the super-squirrel, the pavement began to buckle. The parking deck was swaying like a man with an inner ear problem stepping off a roller coaster.

"OK, what's going on?" asked Mark, ducking low and grabbing for the barrier wall.

"Calm down, chief," replied the telekinetic squirrel. "I'm taking out the campus generator. You said there were a bunch of Hollow Men pushing a wheel right below it, right?"

Timmy stood authoritatively atop the wall, his cape fluttering behind him. He nodded his tiny head toward the center of the WANG campus and thought. He thought his motherfucking brains out. Figuratively, of course. Timmy's brains were, literally, still very much inside of his head and, in fact, responsible for all the thinking.

An engine of conjoined semicircular induction apparatuses, about the size of a small park, began to dent and shake on the far side of the main building. The concrete beneath the generator started to crack and fall away, into the Hollow Earth, while the generator itself was lifted several feet into the air.

"Couldn't you have waited until we got back down to street level?" asked Mark, gripping the edge of the parking deck with white knuckles. Behind him, the RV slid sideways slightly.

"I wouldn't be able to see anything from there," explained Timmy, never removing his focus from the mangled engine. "In case you haven't noticed it, I'm not very tall."

The cape-wearing squirrel hurled the massive generator into the main building of WANG Electric with his brain.

"You know that wasn't part of the plan, Timmy!" shouted Mark above the sounds of the WANG corporate headquarters collapsing behind a cloud of dust. "The plan was to come up with a new plan!"

"This was the new plan," the rodent replied coolly. "I came up with it just now, when I did it."

"We said we were going to talk it over!"

"You would've told me not to do it!"

CHAPTER SIXTY-FIVE:
WHAT WOULD YOU DO
IF I SANG OUT OF TUNE?

THOR ODINSON, DESPITE HIS LACK of book learnin', was far, far too arrogant to ever be possessed by a ghost. "Typhoid" Mary Mallon had made a valiant effort – her own sense of self-worth on par with that of Donald Trump – but was almost immediately sent careening back out of the thunder god's body, clutching at her see-through head. The Norse god escaped with only a terrific migraine. Tanner the silverback gorilla, however, had a lot of issues with her self-image and was easily overpowered by the psychopathic compulsions of Lizbeth "Lizzie" Borden. This was why the gorilla was currently straddling Thor's midsection, pinning him to the cracking concrete and beating the ever-loving shit out of the thunder god.

Thor, unable to think or see straight, and desperately trying not to throw up, wasn't putting up much of a fight. In fact, he was mostly just bleeding. And getting punched in the face by a great ape possessed by an axe-murderer who hadn't gotten any saner over the last two hundred years. He lifted his arms over his face and tried to shimmy out from under Tanner, kicking his way backward until his head and shoulders were pressed against the side of a transformer. There was a terrific wrenching sound and then the Norseman felt himself fall back onto a row of jagged metal. Wincing through the pain, he could have sworn he saw the transformer hovering over him. Then it disappeared. Then he was in pain. Then it was over him again. Then it disappeared. Then pain.

The cycle repeated itself a few times before Thor realized that the gorilla was savagely beating him with one of the macro-transformers.

"Quit it," he slurred quietly, his mouth full of blood. "Tha's not... tha's not... cool..."

The car-sized electrical device clobbered him once more.

Thor began to black out.

Lucky for him, though, he had friends.

Even luckier for him, those friends had friends of their own that were thoroughly prepared for random assaults by gorillas possessed by homicidal grandmas.

A half pound of iodized salt came flying through the air, landing squarely in Tanner's face. The ghost of "Lizzie" Borden recoiled at the contact, her ethereal form jumping from the gorilla like a sudsed-up naked person in the shower from a spider. Tanner, for her part, fell mewling to the ground, pawing salt out of her eyes. The transformer dropped once more onto Thor before toppling to the side.

Another handful of salt sailed through the faces and torsos of the writhing ghosts. The visages of the old women shuddered and distorted –

"Oh dear," said "Typhoid" Mary Mallon.

– then blinked out of existence altogether, before the final grain of salt hit the ground.

Thor and Tanner, heads still spinning, turned awkwardly and looked up through teary, swollen eyes. The shadowy figures of Chester A. Arthur XVII, Queen Victoria XXX, and Martin Van Buren XCIX, backlit by the brilliant sun, towered over them.

"Hey, guys," Thor said weakly. "New guy. How'd you know there were gonna be ghosts?"

"I didn't," said Martin Van Buren XCIX. "But I carry salt around at all times for emergencies." He patted the satchel hanging near his waist. "I've got a flare gun, a first aid kit, beef jerky –"

"Beef jerky?"

"— powdered water, an elephant whistle, a towel... You guys don't keep stuff like that on you?"

"I have a revolver and a couple knives," said Queen Victoria XXX, putting a hand on her thigh. "Plus I have a camera that needs charging in my backpack," she continued. "Which I think I might have left in New London."

Thor – having removed himself from the jagged metal foundation of the transformer and sprawled on his back on an altogether more comfortable section of concrete – pulled a hand from the pocket of his jeans and said, "I've got a Buy One/Get One Free coupon for that steak place outside Cretaceous Park. And an 'Inspected by Inspector 42' sticker."

The clone of the eighth president turned toward that of the twenty-first with his brow knit. Chester A. Arthur XVII shrugged in reply.

"I don't even have my own clothes right now," he said, lightly lifting his leather jacket from his abdomen. "You didn't exactly catch us at our best moment."

Martin Van Buren XCIX stood there, staring at them, a look of bemusement on his face. After a minute he said, "Billy always goes on and on about how good you guys are at this stuff."

"We are," replied Chester A. Arthur XVII indignantly.

"Just not always on purpose," added Queen Victoria XXX.

CHAPTER SIXTY-SIX:
BLOOD, SWEAT, AND TEARS

WILLIAM H. TAFT XLII RUSHED INTO the primary control room, a left-handed spork-head screwdriver in his outstretched hand. Dr. Lee Arahami and Bio-Evocative Technologist X1211MR, sitting on the floor in a tangle of wires, turned from the diagnostic program running on the roboticist's tablet to look at the president. Queen Victoria XXX, sitting in a chair nearby, glanced up from the ten-year-old copy of *Wired* she had found in the bathroom.

"We got the screwdriver," gasped the fat man, promptly doubling over and placing his hands on his knees.

The cloned president had been followed into the room by Boudica IX, the Celtic queen smiling and wearing a lion fur as a cloak. She also had the top half of a lion's skull on her head.

"They made me their queen," she said giddily.

The scientists and the other cloned queen looked at Boudica IX with concern in their eyebrows.

"We'll explain later," huffed William H. Taft XLII, finally almost catching his breath. "Where's everyone else?"

"Charlie and Marty are installing the trivection cooling unit," answered Bex. "Tanner and Thor are out replacing the substation macro-transformers damaged by the old ladies wearing the giant sloths."

The reconstituted politician looked at the robot scientist with his eyebrow raised.

"We'll explain later," said Queen Victoria XXX.

"The screwdriver, Billy?" said Bex, holding out her hand. "We've still got work to do on the regulators."

"Do you want me to give you a hand with that?" asked Dr. Arahami.

"I'm sure I can handle it by myself."

"Well, yeah, but..."

"But?"

"I came all this way..."

The HEART inside the lady robot analyzed the scientist's tone of voice, performed several thousand analyses, and then dinged, all in the span of a microsecond.

"OK, fine," she said, standing and brushing off wire. "You can help."

Bex sashayed out the rear door of the primary control room, onto the electrical grid. Dr. Arahami, after a moment, unplugged his tablet with unprecedented gusto and raced after the technologist.

"I don't get why everyone's in such a rush to get this done," mumbled Queen Victoria XXX, turning back to her magazine.

"Well, let's see..." said William H. Taft XLII with considerably serrated sarcasm. "Communications are still down, food is going bad left and right, businesses are failing, most of the dinosaurs broke out of Cretaceous Park, poor people are looting, rich people are devolving into darkness-fearing asshats, and there's no *Two and a Half Men* repeats to placate the dumb ones and keep them from procreating.

"Seriously, Vicky," he continued, "every second the blackout continues, Las Vegas – hell, everyone everywhere – moves one step closer to scratching off their own skin like a detoxing meth addict dropped in a vat of chile peppers. I didn't see it until recently, but a lot of those people out there, the ones who aren't us, the ones who weren't genetically bred to fix this, the ones who've put up with this shit for *decades*, they are *fucked up* and it takes every nicety and distraction ever invented to just barely keep them civil."

"Oh, right, yeah," said the queen, nodding complacently. "Other people. That sounds exhausting."

"It is."

"You ever miss just goofing off with us?"

"Not really, no," said the mayor-king of Las Vegas. "When you and Charlie weren't fucking on the couch I wanted to watch TV on, you were making fun of me."

"We did do that a lot, didn't we?"

"You guys *are* kind of buttholes sometimes," said Boudica IX.

"I don't think buttholes is the word you're looking for."

"No, she means buttholes," replied William H. Taft XLII.

***

Some time later, Thor Odinson and Tanner the silverback gorilla returned to the primary control room, drenched in sweat and covered in grease. The scientists were sitting in the only two chairs in the room making idle chit chat, while Chester A. Arthur XVII and Martin Van Buren XCIX were slumped in the corner and still covered in perspiration, having just returned themselves. Queen Victoria XXX and William H. Taft XLII were standing nearby, looking bored and anxious, respectively.

Boudica IX, meanwhile, was curled up in her lion fur, sleeping a few feet outside the control room door. She had farted and was forcefully removed from the room after everyone regained consciousness.

The thunder god walked over to where Dr. Arahami was sitting, picked up the scientist, placed him on the ground, and then slumped into his chair with such tremendous exhaustion that the floor shook slightly. The gorilla did the same, only she moved Bex.

Leaning his head back against the top of the chair, Thor exhaled deeply. Then he said, "Well, that's done."

"That part of it, yes," agreed Dr. Arahami.

"What do you mean, 'that part of it?'" Thor leaned forward in the chair.

"We still have to restart the perpetual motion engine," explained Chester A. Arthur XVII from the corner. "And by we, I mean you. It's going to require an inordinate amount of electrical energy. Enough to kill the rest of us if we even get within a few miles."

"I have to go back out there?" whined Thor, pointing a thumb toward the door. "You do remember this thing is a giant fucking state, right? We were out there for, like, days."

"The engine isn't that far," said Martin Van Buren XCIX. "Comparatively."

"Comparatively to what?"

"It's not like you have to walk it," said Queen Victoria XXX.

"There's a Segway in the closet," continued William H. Taft XLII.

"A fucking scooter?" muttered Thor.

"The sooner you do it, the sooner we can all leave," added Dr. Arahami.

"This is bullshit."

Slowly, begrudgingly, exhaustedly, the thunder god peeled himself from the chair and shuffled to the closet. He pulled the Segway free and held it in his hands.

"Is this because of what I did to your truck?" Thor asked the roboticist. "We can totally get that stain out."

The roboticist walked over to the Segway and started pushing buttons on the mounted directional pad.

"There," he said, after a moment. "It's programmed to take you there automatically. All you have to do is stand on it."

"Staaaand?" whined the thunder god.

CHAPTER SIXTY-SEVEN: ONE BABY ASPIRIN AND HE'LL BE OUT FOR DAYS

AFTER DISMANTLING THE GENERATOR for the WANG Electric corporate campus, as well as much of the WANG Electric campus itself, Mark Hughes and Timmy the super-squirrel were forced to flee with great abandon. Neither of them had counted on the company having a fleet of battery-operated drones at its disposal, nor did they expect the drones to have a seemingly infinite supply of small, projectile explosives. With Timmy too exhausted to think and Mark without a pie tin, the duo was forced to engage in a much more time-tested option of not getting shot in the face by flying killer robots.

They hopped in their RV and drove the fuck out of Atlanta.

"So what do we do now?"

"What do you mean, 'what do we do now?' We keep driving the hell away from there," said Timmy. "Maybe get some more pie."

"We should probably tell Thor and Charlie about what went down," said Mark, flooring the RV north on the ruined pavement of I-95. "Right? That's generally the next step?"

"The only thing I'm wearing is a cape. Where would I keep a phone? Besides, we're done. WANG is ruined, a tiny, shriveled, useless nub of what it used to be. I think this'll keep until we see them again."

"Yeah... About that, Timmy... When we were fleeing, I, uh, I saw a sign. Turns out WANG Electric is a subsidiary of the Walt Sidney Company."

"The Walt Sidney Company? The largest, most beloved, most vengeful corporation on Earth? That's... that's great, Mark." The tiny squirrel slumped back into the passenger seat.

"All in the name of being a hero, right? Helping the less fortunate with no regard for our own person well-being? The Hollow Men are certainly –"

"Holy shit, man, can we talk about this later?" snapped the psychic rodent. "I just committed an act of domestic terrorism with my *brain*. My head is killing me."

"Oh, right. Sorry."

"'Sorry.' Frigging normals," thought Timmy quietly. "'Thinking doesn't take any effort, let's talk!' Yeah, well, you try lifting ten tons of metal with your mind."

"I said sorry."

Timmy the super-squirrel pulled his cape over his head and began drifting off to sleep, grumbling the entire way.

CHAPTER SIXTY-EIGHT:
CTRL + ALT + DELETE

A FEW HOURS LATER, THOR, having found an extremely uncomfortable position in which he could sleep on the scooter, woke with a start as the Segway stopped and threw him to the ground. He was on the edge of a rectangular depression, white concrete sloping downward to a hulking electric motor the size of an office building. Enormous industrial fans were situated in the ground and angled walls surrounding the machine. A number of trailer home-sized generators were lined along the opposite lip of the depression.

"I guess this is it," said Thor. He looked around for a sign confirming his suspicion, then quickly stopped giving a crap.

Taking a few slow, deep breaths, the thunder god raised his hands to the sky. This in and of itself didn't do anything, but he thought it would look cool.

The blinding sunlight was quickly drowned out as black clouds rolled in from one end of the horizon to the other. Thunder rumbled tremendously – above, below, everywhere – shaking the concrete surrounding Thor and sending shivers through every piece of industrial machinery within two miles. Hundreds of bolts of lightning began to light up the air, crisscrossing the sky and weaving tighter and tighter together. Within moments, the crosshatched lightning closed and converged, and a single titanic thunderbolt seared through the ether and into the perpetual motion engine.

As the lightning dissipated and the clouds began to part, Thor could hear the dull whirring mechanics of the motor and the generators kicking back to life. Beyond them, lines of lampposts and the LEDs of machines flickered and flashed back on.

"Holy crap," said the thunder god, "it actually worked."

Thor marveled at the machinery for only a moment, as his keen sense of when other people were eating without him kicked in. He felt a sudden need to get back to the primary control room as quickly as inhumanly possible.

The Norseman undid his belt and tied it around the Segway. Having slept through most of the trip out to the engine, Thor wasn't entirely sure which way the control room was — not that this was going to stop him. The thunder god searched the horizon, picked a direction on a hunch, and shrugged. He cocked his arm back.

"I hope I don't land on anything important."

CHAPTER SIXTY-NINE:
SPITE. IT'S WHAT'S FOR DINNER

CATRINA DALISAY AND ALI ŞAHIN stumbled into the control room, struggling for both air and the ability to stand up straight. The clones, the scientists, the god, and the gorilla, huddled around two chairs and a plank of plywood serving as a makeshift dining table, turned to the returning couple with looks more of mild curiosity than any kind of actual concern.

"We... we got..." gasped Ali, his face somewhere around his knees, "the isotonium." The messenger bag hanging from his shoulder glowed slightly.

"We ran... all the way here," added Catrina, before leaning back out of the doorway and vomiting daintily.

"Oh, good for you," said Dr. Arahami from behind a mouthful of cheeseburger. "We'll put the ore in the storage shed with the rest of it, in case we need it later."

"What?" asked Catrina groggily, leaning her back against the doorframe and wiping her mouth. Ali sat at her feet staring at the roboticist.

"We're done, guys," said Chester A. Arthur XVII. "We've repaired everything and the continental electrical grid is back online. Society is well on its way back to forgetting any of this ever happened." He held out a greasy bag. "Burger?"

"Fuck all of you," said Catrina exhaustedly, raising both middle fingers, although not far and not at anyone in particular.

"We're not helping you anymore," added Ali. He removed the messenger bag containing the isotonium and slid it towards the scientists. "But we will eat your food."

The brown-skinned man climbed to his knees, reached up, and snatched the bag from the cloned president. He immediately slumped back down to the ground and leaned his back against the wall. Catrina stumbled over, falling to her knees, and then her ass, miraculously ending up in a sitting position next to her boyfriend. The two tore into the burgers with a ferocity usually reserved for caged zoo animals and children lost for weeks in the wilderness.

"Wait, where's my car?" asked Chester A. Arthur XVII.

CHAPTER SEVENTY: HAPPY ENDINGS

CHESTER A. ARTHUR XVII AND Martin Van Buren XCIX shook heartily, gripping each other's hands forcefully and for maybe a moment or two too long.

"It was good seeing you again, Marty," said the dead president.

"You too, Charlie," said the other dead president. They were standing, still clasping hands, on the large lot of cracked asphalt outside the primary control room of Montana. The rest of their friends were likewise milling around the parking lot, saying their goodbyes, packing their scant possessions up, and trying to figure out seating arrangements for the long rides home.

"You sure you don't want to come back to Las Vegas with us?" continued Martin Van Buren XCIX. "I'm sure Billy can get you a lucrative position in City-State Hall. I think Viceroy of Lounge Acts is open."

"Thanks, but we tried that once[31]. I think we're all better off if I stay in Secaucus."

"You sure you guys don't want to fuck in the bathroom?" asked Queen Victoria XXX, barging over and placing her hands on theirs. "You know, for old times' sake?"

"I think we're all right," said Chester A. Arthur XVII.

"We don't want to ruin that magic moment," added Martin Van Buren XCIX.

"Fine," replied the former British monarch with an eye roll and a flamboyant sigh. She let go of the men's hands, and they finally did the same.

Turning on her heel, the cloned queen saw William H. Taft XLII exiting down the cargo bay ramp of his enormous, multi-engine long-range helicopter, having pulled his glorified dune buggy into the hold.

"You riding as co-pilot, Bex?" the large man called into the crowd. He slid a pair of modified welding goggles over his head.

"Actually, yes," replied the robot, "but not with you."

"What?"

"I'm going back to Lee's volcano lair for a while," she continued. "To... help. With things."

"Sex things," clarified Thor, still not wearing pants, having once again lost his jeans while attempting to "fly."

"If you're going to get technical, sure."

"I'll ride with you, Billy!" chirped Boudica IX, raising her hand, her sweater sliding down her arm.

It was now Thor's turn to ask, "What?"

"I thought we should start seeing other people," the redheaded clone explained, grabbing her bag from the ground. "A couple days ago, actually. This seemed like a good time to tell you about it."

"But, pumpkinhead –"

"Sorry, sugarpubes," she said, stepping over and lightly kissing him on the cheek, "but you're not as heavy as you used to be and I don't like it."

"I could eat more."

"There's also our mutual lack of actual concern for one another."

"But mutual is good," said the crestfallen Norseman.

"I'm sorry, Thor." The queen placed a hand on his shoulder. "But I'm just not that into you."

Thor nodded slightly, a look of rueful acceptance set on his face. Then he leaned in gently and whispered, "Speaking of 'into you,' is your vajajay working right now?"

Boudica IX reached a hand under her skirt and said, "Think so."

"Quickie in the bathroom before you go? You know, for the road?"

"Yeah, all right."

The two immediately raced back into the primary control room, pulling their clothes off as they went. Catrina, watching with her face scrunched in vague confusion and mild distaste, turned to look at William H. Taft XLII. The mayor-king shrugged nonchalantly.

"See?" barked Queen Victoria XXX, looking toward the cloned presidents and pointing toward the god and the redhead. "They know how to say goodbye!"

"We're not having sex again, Vicky," replied Chester A. Arthur XVII sternly.

"Come on, one more time. Do him for me."

"Tyrone's sending us all a copy of the movie," said Martin Van Buren XCIX. "You'll probably have it in your email as soon as you get home."

"But that could be days!" the queen whined.

While Queen Victoria XXX made one final attempt to get her friends to bang one another, Tanner the silverback gorilla sidled up next to Catrina, sliding off her headphones.

"Excuse me, hi," began the gorilla. "Do you have any idea how long Thor and your redheaded friend are going to be in there? Those burgers are ripping right through me."

"Oh, uh, I don't know," stammered the clerk. "Probably a while."

"All right, thanks," muttered Tanner, biting her lip. She spotted a modestly-sized clump of scrubby shrubbery growing through the asphalt and made for it, then settled in and noisily began taking care of business. Bex and Dr. Arahami, talking nerdy to one another only a few feet from the gorilla, either didn't notice or didn't care.

Ali, silent witness to all of the preceding, stepped behind Catrina and began gently rubbing her shoulders.

"We've really got to find some new friends," he said.

"That is priority number one when we get home."

***

Early the next morning, after taking shifts and driving straight through the night, Dr. Arahami's all-terrain tractor-trailer finally arrived at the custom luxury-tank of Chester A. Arthur XVII and the patch of lonely desert surrounding it.

The truck idling, Chester A. Arthur XVII was the last to step from the back of the tractor-trailer, turning and pulling the retractable door shut as he exited. He stepped to the side of the trailer and waved into the large rearview mirror of the truck cab.

"Thanks again, Lee, for –"

The president was met with a half-assedly waving hand shoved out of the window and a faceful of mildly radioactive exhaust. He began coughing violently, placing his hands on his knees. Queen Victoria XXX hurried over and began rubbing his back.

"He *really* wants to hump that robot," she said, watching the truck vanish into the distance.

"You guys might want to stand back," said Thor, hunching near the methane port on the side of the custom-built tank and dropping his boxers. "I've been holding this in since New Hollywood."

***

Several days later, Chester A. Arthur XVII, Queen Victoria XXX, Thor Odinson, Catrina Dalisay, and Ali Şahin arrived at the burned down pile of rubble that used to be the Secaucus Holiday Inn. Beyond the ashes, the entire Plaza at the Meadows could be seen, completely abandoned.

"We probably should have remembered this," said Catrina, climbing from the luxury-tank and surveying the damage.

"Remembered what? What happened?" queried Chester A. Arthur XVII, knitting his brow. "I seem to be missing a good chunk of the days between Vicky strapping me to a hand cart and when I ended up on Joselin's operating table."

"We'll explain later, honey," replied Queen Victoria XXX, leaning into her boyfriend and sliding a hand into the back pocket of his trousers. "It involves you dying a lot."

"We should probably find a new home, right?" asked Ali. "That should probably be a thing we're concerned about?"

"I think I'd rather go get pancakes," said Thor.

"I think I'd rather do that too," echoed Catrina.

"I could eat," added Chester A. Arthur XVII.

"We should probably get Thor some new pants first," offered Queen Victoria XXX, surveying the large blonde man in the flannel shirt, work boots, and heart-covered boxer shorts.

"There's no time for pants, woman," said the thunder god. Pointing a finger into the air, he shouted, "To the diner!"

ACKNOWLEDGMENTS

THANKS TO MONICA, MIKE, STEVE, Sarita, and assorted friends and family; Douglas Adams and Kurt Vonnegut; classic rock, old Marvel comics, Cracked.com, *Community* and most assuredly *Futurama*; Jamaican ginger ale, Pringles salt and vinegar chips, and Blake's green chile cheeseburgers; and, last but not least, coffee.

I love you, coffee.

ABOUT THE AUTHOR

Eirik Gumeny is over six feet tall and enjoys sugar. Originally from the highway-choked suburbs of New Jersey, he now lives in the mile-high desert of New Mexico. He is very pale and it is very sunny, so he will probably combust any day now.

Eirik has often been told his work is most likely influenced by drugs, an excessive intake of coffee, or a lack of sleep, but he'd prefer to blame Douglas Adams, Kurt Vonnegut, Warren Zevon, and the many hours he's spent watching *Futurama*.

Eirik is the author of the *Exponential Apocalypse* series and the founding/former editor of *Jersey Devil Press*. He co-authored *Screw the Universe* with Stephen Schwegler and has been featured in several post-apocalyptic and bizarro anthologies. His short fiction has been collected in the e-book *We're Going to Die Here, Aren't We?* and his flash fiction has been published in two chapbooks, *Storybook Romance* and *Boy Meets Girl*. His plays have been workshopped in New York City, his resumes have gotten a number of his friends jobs, and his doodles occasionally make it onto the refrigerator.

Eirik has never been awarded a Pushcart, though he has twice been nominated for one. He's also never won a Nobel Prize, a Pulitzer, an Olympic medal, or the NFC East. He did win a camera at work once, though. When Eirik is not writing or daydreaming about being on his book tour with his wife, he's probably asleep and actually dreaming about it. Or in his living room teaching his dog it's OK to chew on shoes.

For more of Eirik's writing go to your computer and navigate your way to egumeny.com. To offer him huge sums of money, email him at eirik.gumeny@gmail.com.

ALSO BY THE AUTHOR

ENDNOTES

---

[1] Both Switzerland and Canada had declared themselves "the friendliest nation on Earth." They held a summit to decide things once and for all. It ended badly.

[2] Sometime between the First Robot War ending the world for the ninth time and the Second Robot War ending the world for the tenth time, the region of New England – under the assumption that robots couldn't climb trees – burned itself to the ground wholesale, planted a majestic, fast-acting Qwik-Wood™ redwood forest in the ashes, and moved their civilization high into the treetops. The important parts, anyway: highways, police stations, Catholic churches, liquor stores. All of it, up there balancing on planks and ropes and spanning the thickest branches, like the jury-rigged treehouse of a twelve-year-old who laughed in, and then peed on, the face of death.

[3] Shortly after sort of saving the world from Andrew Jackson II and Nikola Tesla's doomsday machine (*Dead Presidents*), Chester A. Arthur XVII and Queen Victoria XXX – fuck buddies and best friends for several years – had an adult conversation about their relationship and tried to give it an honest go. The conversation, and the ensuing relationship, involved a lot of hemming, hawing, and dancing around words like "love," but eventually they figured it out.

[4] A few months earlier, Ali spend time with Dr. Arahami, recuperating from a broken ankle. While resting at his volcano lair, the mad scientist was able to talk Ali into converting over to a pneumatic penis. A kind of harnessed enhancement, comprised of compressed air and physical sensors, the dong survived the solar storm without a problem. (*Dead Presidents*)

[5] Shortly after the world was ended for the eleventh time, the first dinosaurs were cloned in what was then the archeological stronghold of Montana. Almost immediately, those first dinosaurs ate their creators. Eventually, the escaped no-longer-extinct reptiles made their way east and settled into Old Maryland, being huge fans of both Baltimore Harbor and meat that couldn't fight back or run away.

[6] The grid was originally consolidated and run by the Amalgamated Provinces and States of Canada, America, and Mexico, a government that had since exploded. (*Exponential Apocalypse*) In its absence, the grid just kept running and the people just kept using it.

[7] Cash money had been thoroughly and completely destroyed several apocalypses earlier.

[8] She was adorably and innocently describing a gender-swapped blumpkin, three things which have never once been said about a blumpkin. For the love of all that is holy, do not Google it.

[9] The wendigo was a hulking creature vaguely in the shape of a human, but mostly claws and teeth and ragged white fur – picture an abominable snowman on meth. According to Native American lore, a human would turn into one after eating the flesh of another human. This would certainly explain why so many wendigo began popping up after the Cannibal Season began.

[10] Even if anyone had known an electrician, it would have been for naught. Most of the world's electricians died twenty months prior, when Quetzalcoatl attacked Las Vegas and turned a construction workers convention into a flaming hell of dismembered foremen and blue-collar unionists. (*Exponential Apocalypse*) Those that survived only milked an extra year from the grim reaper's teat, as the cruise they chartered for the one year anniversary of the Las Vegas massacre lost power within days of leaving port and the workers were forced to eat one another for sustenance. The last man made it to his own waist before he bled to death.

[11] Shortly after the world ended for the twenty-fourth time and the citizens of the United Provinces and States of America, Canada, and Mexico voted in a democratically-elected anarchy as their government, states and provinces as they were once known slowly dissolved. After a while, the only constituently administrated organizations left were a handful of corporate-owned city-states and some globally-acknowledged independent territories.

[12] Formerly New Mexico, Arizona, and small chunks of Nevada and southern California, Las Máquinas was ceded to the robots in appeasement following the Third Robot War. The territory was also home to a large number of scientists, stranded amidst the vengeful automatons thanks to a failed political reign and a spiteful populace. (*Dead Presidents* has more information.)

[13] In Norse mythology, the realm of the frost giants.

[14] Known variously as wood nymphs, dryads, or sprites, the woodfolk were a previously mythic race of sexy green people who lived in the forest, alternately seducing, assisting, or causing problems for humans, and generally acting exactly like one would expect a race of sexy green people who lived in the forest to act.

[15] For a brief period following the world ending for the fourth time, there was no internet. This made some people very sad and confused, and others very angry. In Sweden, particularly, many online citizens took the loss of the world wide web as a personal attack and started to attack everyone and everything they could find personally. After blighting all opposing viewpoints in their own country – even the ones whose opposition consisted solely of "Please don't hurt me" – the Swedish

Torrenters, as they called themselves, set their sights on Norway, much to the chagrin of the burgeoning Neo-Viking movement there. It did not take long for this to devolve into a full-scale ideological war, ultimately resulting in both countries being set on fire. They stayed that way for many, many years, as Scandinavia was apparently an excellent source of fuel.

[16] The extinct animal sanctuary built over what used to be Oklahoma.

[17] Mark's ocular implant ran off a small atomic battery and was not affected by the geomagnetic superstorm at all. The mechanical eye was, however, affected by his sobriety, or, more specifically, his lack thereof. The implant had earlier been knocked offline due to Mark's spending most of the early days of the blackout blind stinking drunk.

[18] The manticore was a creature previously thought to be found only in ancient Persian mythology. The beast had the body of the lion, the head of a man, and the tail of a scorpion. When a manticore mauled – or poisoned – someone it got rid of all the evidence: the skin, the bones, anything the victim was carrying. It was the Walter White of mythological monsters.

[19] The Jersey Devil is a fearsome beast said to have been birthed by Deborah Leeds in the 1700s. Born human, it immediately changed into some kind of demon-looking thing and flew out into the night where it has terrorized New Jersey and the surrounding areas for centuries. By most accounts, the creature walks upright on thick legs and cloven hooves, has the head of a horse, the wings of a bat, and the tail of a cartoon devil.

[20] The Mexican goatsucker. A cross between a feral dog and a lizard, chupacabra travel in packs, prey mainly on livestock, and don't take kindly to being disturbed.

[21] The Hawaiian volcano goddess.

[22] Like a tyrannosaurus rex, only bigger and meaner.

[23] After being decimated during the fourth end of the world, Atlanta rebuilt and was now one of the largest city-states on the continent, expanding its metropolis to include all of what used to be Georgia, most of what was once South Carolina, and the parts of the former state of Florida that hadn't sunk into the ocean.

[24] A mythical Arabic bird of prey possessed of enormous size and strength. Like, seriously enormous. Rocs ate elephants like M&Ms.

[25] Alcatraz had been abandoned several years earlier, along with the rest of San Francisco. That did not mean that the inmates had been moved, or even that they weren't have a grand old time. The thing about letting inmates run the asylum is that the inmates tend to enjoy it a lot more that way.

[26] The vast majority of the world's economy was credit-based after Mars fell into the sun and an intense heat wave burned up all the physical money on the planet. People could still barter for goods, but people were kind of selfish jerkfaces.

[27] See the original *Exponential Apocalypse* for more details.

[28] Back in the days before science got all up on religion's jock, if a person was bad and then died, that person went to Hell (or their religion's version of it). If someone was really bad, that person went to Hell and was promoted to a demon, a title that granted them some prestige and power but ultimately meant little, much like how most corporations are 25% vice presidents. When religion was disproven, those demons – like the gods, angels, and Satan himself – were made mortal and stripped of any underworldly powers they might have had, and now worked for minimum wage.

[29] "**ruth**, noun, pronounced *rooth*: A feeling of sympathy and sorrow for the misfortunes of others." Bet you wish you had a Kindle right now.

[30] Dr. Lee Arahami created the first artificially sentient robot. As such, when the robots rebelled years later, the media and the government saddled him and him alone with the burden of being humanity's downfall. Because finding a scapegoat is a lot easier than trying to understand differing viewpoints and complex scientific words and stuff.

[31] William H. Taft XLII, shortly after being crowned mayor-king, hired Thor as the sole bouncer for Las Vegas and appointed Chester A. Arthur XVII as the security director for the casino syndicate. They were let go in short order, however, as Charlie wasn't so much looking out for card sharks as he was learning from them. It also didn't help that Thor slept with one of William H. Taft XLII's ex-hooker wives.